FABULOUS TRICKS

Blue Snow, winner of a *Gay Scotland* short story competition, was first published in *Gay Scotland*; *Filipino Sting* was originally published in *Gay Times*.

FABULOUS TRICKS

Stories by Gay Men

Edited by

David Rees, Peter Robins, and Dave Royle

THIRD HOUSE (Publishers)

First published in 1992 by Third House (Publishers),
69 Regent Street, Exeter EX2 9EG, England

World copyright on the collection © Third House
(Publishers) 1992; on each individual work © the author
1992

Story editors: David Rees, Peter Robins, Dave Royle
ISBN I 870188 I8 7

Typeset by Bookman Ltd, 2c Merrywood Road,
Bristol BS3 1DX

Distributed in the British Isles and Europe by Turnaround
Distribution, 27 Horsell Road, London, N5 1XL

Distributed in North America by InBook,
140 Commerce Street, East Haven, Connecticut 06512,
U.S.A.

Distributed in Australia and New Zealand by
Stilone pty, Ltd., P.O. Box 155, Broadway, New South
Wales 2007, Australia

Printed and bound in Great Britain by
Billing and Sons Ltd, Worcester

CONTENTS

BREAKFAST SERVED ALL DAY

Toby Manning

Walking through the early morning streets, Karl remembered again just how much he enjoyed this tired but invigorating feeling of the morning after. How much he enjoyed returning home from some unfamiliar part of town that he would not be able to find again, or even remember very clearly! He liked being out on the streets as people were only just setting off for work, when the traffic had not yet picked up its full momentum. This was a luxury, to be able just to enjoy the morning when the day was that little bit more intimate, before the anonymity of the rush hour.

There were tramps coming back from their night-spots under bridges out early to look for cigarette butts dropped the night before; obsessive businessmen rushing out early to make the biggest killing, shaving as they sped by in their BMWs. Grumpy, bleary-eyed truckers and all-night drivers sitting in the roadside caffs over huge steaming mugs of tea and griddled breakfasts in places that bore *Breakfast served all day* signs.

And perhaps there were a few others like himself making tracks back home after a long night. Hungered by sex, frustrated desire, or alcohol. Red-eyed and jumpy. Sore and dry, but still ticking over until the fuse fizzled out. This particular day was one of those cold, bright days when winter phases into spring. The sky was crisp and starched bluey-white over the clear lines of the buildings. The sun seemed to be redefining those lines, giving the buildings shape and texture that the drizzling winter months had fuzzed and

1

distorted. Flowers sprang up in window-boxes; grass that had been flattened by winter stood up, and tower blocks, church spires, chimneys and cranes seemed to reassert themselves against the skyline.

Karl inhaled the air about him. The scent of the man he had spent the night with still lingered about his body like fingers touching and caressing him lightly beneath his clothes. His skin was sensitive, and those imaginary fingers made it tighten and tingle as he walked on through the morning's strengthening sunlight. And as he passed people on the street he thought to himself, I wonder if you have any idea where I have been: what I've been doing. What would you think if you knew whose hands I can feel over my body right now. . .

The long streets of garages and cafés near the ring road moved behind him and gave way to the criss-cross of canals and railway tracks of the town centre. As he passed under the railway arch he saw that there were already early morning hopefuls waiting by the public toilets. He turned away from them.

But somebody was calling him. 'Hey mate!'

He looked round.

'Hey mate! I like your jacket!'

On the corner near the toilets stood a middle-aged man. Karl knew him by sight. He'd seen him in bars – ridiculously out of place – trying to engage younger, prettier men in conversation. On his parents' terms you might invite him round for tea, but there was something shabby, something seedy, about him. Perhaps it was just that his loneliness was too visible. Karl carried on down the street.

The man followed, calling after him. 'Can't you spare five minutes for a chat then?'

Karl relented slightly. 'I'm catching a bus.'

'That's better.' The man drew level, asking 'What's your name?'

Karl grew impatient. 'Does it matter?' He started to move off again.

'I just like you that's all.' He paused. 'I like your eyes.'

Karl couldn't help blushing. 'Look, sorry; I've got to go – you've got the wrong bloke.' He moved off, quicker this time.

2

The man called after him, insistently. 'I like you. Pity you can't stop. . .'

Karl kept moving, thinking, you've got the wrong bloke . . . It's not me you want.

He remembered a time when he was stuck in a station, waiting for a connecting train. He was lying on a bench restlessly trying to sleep but was kept awake by the nervous laughter of a rent boy and a tramp sharing a drink at a kiosk. The rent boy was clumsy; he kept spilling his beer onto his white shirt. He bought the tramp a drink, stroking his right arm as if it ached, as he paid. It must have been a hard night. Tired of watching them comparing their tattoos, Karl went to take a leak. A slight figure emerged from the shadows and squeezed into the urinal with him. He pushed him away with an expression of disgust. The man thudded against the wash basin, stammering. Karl did up his flies and walked out.

He thought about it now as he walked towards the bus stop. It was moral somehow, that push, implying, I'm not like that. But why not a more honest approach; why not I don't fancy you? Even then that didn't really explain it. Hadn't there been times when drunk enough, lustful enough, and flattered enough he had gone with men he didn't really fancy? What was the difference between picking up a stranger at a club or a party, and meeting one in a toilet? He hated the idea of those men lurking in corners for just a glimpse of flesh or a grope, waiting for their brief moment of cheap sensation. But now he was coming back from his own quest for cheap sensation as if it were intrinsically better. What was the difference?

He went up the stairs on the bus, suddenly conscious again of people around him. Was it visible, this feeling that coursed along his skin? He remembered slipping out early this morning with the man gently breathing, sighing, and turning over. Or had he even stirred? He couldn't now remember. On occasions one of his one-nighters would wake up, but would normally be too bleary to know or be bothered why this lunatic was dressing at seven a.m. Karl had the ability to be completely awake as soon as he opened his eyes; then he would want to be gone, out in the air with the smell of frying bacon and baking bread. The bus was heading for the south side of town, through the centre where the cleaners were still

3

doing their early morning rounds in the department stores. Karl watched them, taking pleasure in their work now that he was on holiday, enjoying his idleness.

There weren't many people on the top deck. He sat down opposite a couple of women on their way to work. They paid no attention to him. They were deep in conversation. Or rather, one of them was. The quiet one was conventionally dressed, in a short, respectable skirt, white blouse; bare-legged, frizzy-haired. But it was the one speaking who caught his attention. She had a slightly haggard, over-sensitive look about her. Her eyes were red at the rims; her face was dark-skinned but pallid-looking. Her hair, bobbed and black, hung untended around her slender neck. Her clothes were more fashionable than her friend's, though based on the same principle.

As his ears adjusted to the hum of the engine, he heard her saying, 'It's just so hard, isn't it?'

If the other woman replied, her reply was registered inaudible by the hiss of gears as the bus picked up speed.

'I mean he's got paranoid now. He's started leaving these little notes around the house, saying "Sorry I haven't done the washing-up." "Sorry I haven't cleaned the bath . . . had to rush out." I don't know if he's taking the piss or what. I mean just because I said I don't see why it all comes down to me. We're both working. I can't face having all the cleaning and stuff to worry about when I come home.'

There was no reply . . . perhaps a grunt of assent.

'It's like you're caught. Between being a drudge and a nag. Men'll have you run round after them, sodding off to the pub whenever they can get away from you, despising you for the way you let yourself be treated. But if you complain, you're the nagging old woman. "Poor old Kev, his Missus gives him a hard time. Won't give him a moment's peace." His mates'll laugh at him, then he'll take it out on you when he gets back, and you feel yourselves growing further and further apart.'

She'd run out of breath, all this having come out in a rush, stopping sometimes agitatedly to look for the right words. Her friend repeated her non-committal noise, looking slightly towards the window at the passing shops, and the windows being wiped down.

4

'It was nice at first,' she began again, 'all romantic and that. But that soon went. He was dead kind to begin with. It seems like years later now, though it's only a few months. It's hard to believe it's the same person. Maybe once they've got used to you they don't feel romantic any more. How many romantic couples do you know who are actually married?' Her friend shrugged and smiled weakly. 'Those couples you see wrapped round each other in Birchfield Park. They're never married, I'll tell you. They'll have been together maybe a few months. Sometimes it just seems like an act to me, just to get you into church and do their washing for them. . . I don't know. Maybe it's the telly that gives us all these daft romantic ideas.' She sighed. 'These last few weeks though, it seems like we can't speak without arguing.'

Karl sat, pretending not to listen, stealing glances every now and then, hearing every word she said. Her friend continued to look out of the window.

'Remember that night I phoned you? I was in a real state. Well, we had it out that night. He seemed to agree. But it was all the same again a few days later. I just can't seem to get through to him. He doesn't see things like me. It's all so simple to him. Sometimes I think he's just waiting for me to shut up.'

Karl wanted to say, 'Look, I know how you feel.' But was it true? He felt sad, and somehow disillusioned. Perhaps it was a comforting thought that elsewhere people were conventionally happy, that life could be simple, cosy. But his idea of normality didn't get far beyond cornflake packets and washing powder commercials. For the third time today an interaction with a stranger had touched him, had triggered responses that normally eluded him. All these people, just looking for somebody to be bothered with for more than five minutes. But could it ever be more than that? Wouldn't it continue to be the strangers that mattered? The strangers whose feelings everyone considered? Karl found it hard to make room for people more intimate than strangers.

The bus arrived in the suburban shopping centre near Karl's home. The two women had got off a few stops further back, heading for an out-of-town office complex. Karl got off the bus and walked along the streets towards home. He was looking

5

forward to eating, to showering. He walked past the unrolling awnings and unbolting doors of the shops. The rush hour had begun, and people pushed him out of the way as they hurried into town. Cars revved their engines, preparing for the morning tail-backs into town. It was all heading away from him.

It had been a long time, a long time since he'd last come home like this; smelling of body and spent energy. This was the nearest he got to cornflake packets, and in truth, the nearest he wanted to get. This way the whole mess of feelings and obligations was kept at arm's length. He could enjoy the intimacy without the intrigue. He was happily compromised between the spoiled cornflake packets and the men outside the public toilets.

He was as independent as the other early risers. Detached as a tramp; self-possessed as the early-bird businessman; self-reliant as a long-distance driver, arriving home from a long run. Opening his front door with a heightened sense of coming home, hanging his jacket on a hook, walking into the kitchen and opening the fridge to take out eggs, bacon, bread and orange juice. He poured himself a glass of juice, put the frying pan on the hot-plate, filled the kettle. Looking up at the clock as he pushed the toast under the grill he saw it was eight thirty, and it felt good to eat now . . . or later . . . or whenever he liked. He had no one to cook for, no one cooking for him, no work to rush off to. He could call this meal breakfast, dinner or tea if he wanted to, for breakfast was served all day every day at his house. It was his decision. He cracked the eggs into the pan and they spat and sizzled as he poured himself a cup of tea.

MASSI

Chris Payne

The cupboard was at the end of a disused corridor at the bottom of the emergency stairs, an area no station refurbishment plan would ever reach. To call it a room would have been an exaggeration. Tony's job paid the rent, and he didn't want to lose it, so he listened cautiously before tapping on the scratched, dark brown door. Inside, there was a soft movement like mice. The door edged open and a face appeared, pink with messy red lipstick, and wispy hair under a tight felt hat.

'Mr Antoniou, have you forgotten my hot chocolate?'

'It's Christmas Eve, remember? You can't stay here locked in all day tomorrow.'

She agreed. 'Where would I have my bath?'

Miss Massey's residence in the cupboard was totally against regulations. Yet those few who knew were more concerned about her becoming homeless again than the certain discipline they would face if she were ever discovered. Fortunately, she was almost invisible. During the day she was out wandering, using the public baths and sitting in the library. She entered and left the station unobtrusively, sometimes at ground level, often by train. When there, it took her several weeks to trust anyone new, and she was particularly suspicious of being seen by the maintenance crews who worked in the tunnels overnight, because they tended to move in crowds and their fluorescent clothing frightened her.

A rare lapse one night the previous summer had caused Tony to discover her. It was well after twelve, and he had been occupied for some time on the southbound platform making sure two drunks went onto a train, not under it. There was only one lift working, and it had just gone; he'd eaten a whole pizza during his break, and remembering Jaz's warnings of what happens when people don't lose weight, he had decided to end his shift by using some calories on the stairs. Only he never made it. Rounding the corner, he almost fell over Miss Massey squatting, having just finished a pee. Politely, he withdrew for a moment, assuming she would make her way to the platform. But after hearing her wheeze off in the other direction, he followed her down the corridor to her cupboard.

How long she had been living there was impossible to know, although the archaeological evidence of her magazines suggested some months. For the rest of the summer and early autumn he and a couple of other staff looked out for her. There were many nights she didn't return, but by October when the cold set in and her chest began to sound like an old goods train going up a hill, she had been back every night. She was increasingly difficult to hide.

In the meantime those who knew the cupboard's secret had begun to adapt to the logic of her view of the world. 'I asked Jaz to put the immersion heater on for you,' Tony said. He helped her on with her coat, which had been hanging on the same hook as a coil of copper wire and a discarded blue overall. 'This coat's damp,' he told her.

'I gave my umbrella to a pair of tourists,' she explained, fastening up the buttons. He could imagine the ceremony with which she had done it, probably in front of a large crowd in Covent Garden.

'You don't look after yourself properly.'

'I'm right as rain,' she said.

There was a stone sink with one tap, some outdated machinery from before the lifts were replaced, Miss Massey's bedding and her carrier bags – all lit by a forty- watt bulb which dangled from a plaited flex.

'I wonder whether you'd be so kind as to carry my Fortnum & Mason for me?' She adjusted her hat. The carriers containing her possessions were also a directory of the capital's élite stores – Bond Street, Knightsbridge and Chelsea. She held four; Tony had one, and two were being left behind. His contained two shapes wrapped in cheap Christmas paper that she would either have charmed or stolen from a street stall.

'Not more stairs!' She gave a dramatic wheeze. The block was shaped like a huge triple sandwich, and its lay-out required that while the door and entrance lobby to the flat were on one level, all the rooms were up the stairs. Jaz looked down at them. He had black hair, brown skin, a black tracksuit with purple flashes and a brilliant white tee-shirt. Miss Massey climbed the stairs laden with bags, looking like a deranged Christmas shopper. Then she put two of them down and offered him her free hand. He dwarfed her. 'Mr Sharma, I've heard so much about you.' She gazed up at his face and stroked his fingers. 'How do you keep your skin so soft?' On the stairs behind her, Tony gave Jaz a nervous glance.

The carrier bags went into the spare bedroom, and the damp coat was hung up to air. She took off her trainers to reveal faded red socks with the heels missing, but her hat accompanied her head into the living room. Jaz noticed the faint smell of cheap soap.

The room had a couple of rugs and lots of lino, a leather three-piece suite and a huge television set from the seventies. Tony wasn't permitted to smoke at work and Jaz wouldn't let him in the car, so he sat down immediately and lit up. She stood at the window, and moved the curtain aside two inches to see the city lights. Away behind the tower blocks, now largely boarded up and unattractive even to squatters, was another tower – Canary Wharf. At street level revellers were singing and slamming car doors, and mothers were leading their children to Midnight Mass.

Miss Massey had to be an early riser in order to emerge from her cupboard before the morning crowds might see her. Christmas Day hadn't dawned when, with a rattling and a teetering, she appeared at Tony's side of the double bed with a tray of tea and toast. 'I warmed the pot,' she assured him, as if two men in the bed was the last thing on her mind.

Tony wriggled up and took the tray. 'This wasn't necessary,'

9

he said, cringing at Jaz's embarrassment. 'Anyway, Happy Christmas, Miss Massey.'

'Happy Christmas, Mr Antoniou and Mr Sharma. I'll have my bath now' (even though she already had her hat and lipstick on.) 'We'll exchange presents after dinner.'

As she closed the door, Tony looked at Jaz. Exposed – naked and homosexual – at six in the morning, he had curled up and turned away. Tony knew it as the "talking back" position. It was able to express hatred, outrage and hurt better than any back he'd known. Being out of work and shunned by his family for living with a man had recently given it too much practice. 'Sorry,' he said, 'She's unpredictable.' The back made no reply. Tony poured two cups of tea. 'Here, might as well make the most of it,' he said through a mouthful of toast, which annoyed Jaz still further. When he had drunk his own he started on the second cup, then finished the toast and went back to sleep until the alarm woke them at nine thirty.

By then Jaz was in a different mood. 'I dreamed some old woman brought us breakfast in the middle of the night.'

Tony was relieved. 'You don't mind her, do you? She'll be gone the day after tomorrow.'

'Course not.' He turned his body towards Tony and there was the movement of hands under the duvet. 'You know what I like best about your body? Your belly. It's firmness.'

'Fat.'

'No. No, really.'

They weren't sexual together very often, and when they were it followed the pattern they had grown used to; perhaps that was what left them both feeling good when they had finished.

Since Jaz had become unemployed his love of cooking had been tainted by the suspicion that he would be seen as the "housewife" against Tony's "breadwinner." However, as nobody was expected to work on Christmas Day he allowed his old enthusiasm back, and kissed Tony when Miss Massey wasn't looking for buying him a Mickey Mouse apron. She had a surprising knowledge of food, and chatted with Jaz as they began preparations for the grand lunch, so that after a little peeling and chopping, Tony sidled out to ring his mum and dad and was forgotten. Later he looked into the kitchen to say he was off in the car to deliver presents to his nephew and niece. Jaz followed him to the staircase, wiping flour off his dark hands onto a cloth.

'Give Elena my love,' he said, positioning Tony's head with one clean finger to kiss his bristly cheek. 'I wonder if any of my brothers or sisters will be in touch. Harbinder might – she sent that birthday card.'

'Don't bank on it. Anyway, at least you two are enjoying yourselves. She's good for you.' In recent times Tony had become very aware of Jaz's moods; it was as hazardous as being a weather forecaster, with the added twist that a down-swing could sometimes be averted if spotted early enough.

'I can't look for work at Christmas, that's all. But she knows her cooking – she was telling me she used to be in service.'

He rejoined Miss Massey, who was rolling pastry.

'Tony loves children. What about you?'

'Oh, I had one once. I was only a girl, unmarried, so Mother and Father had him adopted.' She didn't pause in her rolling movements. Jaz had opened the oven door to check the bird, and the heat blasted his legs. For a second he considered putting a hand on her shoulder, but she didn't seem at all upset. 'Nowadays I'd have jumped the waiting list and got a council flat for it. No, Mr Sharma, I don't like children. They are noisy and boisterous, and very hard work. I was quite content for him to be brought up by some woman who wanted him. You're letting the heat out.'

Jaz closed the oven door and changed the subject to television because he felt awkward with her matter-of-factness. Miss Massey, of course, had little knowledge of recent soap operas, but she turned out to be knowledgeable and quite opinionated on films of the forties and fifties, specialising in minor stars who had killed themselves by jumping from the huge letters that overlooked Hollywood.

From listening inattentively to Tony's descriptions, Jaz had expected their guest to be a helpless geriatric talking nonsense, but he was in fact fascinated and impressed by how much she knew – and she never wasted a word. He also discovered that if he made his responses camp, she was encouraged to talk still more.

'Add a pinch of parsley,' he read from the book propped open against the kettle.

'Don't have any,' she confirmed with a glance towards the shelf (which she had inspected whilst preparing their breakfast) where small glass jars contained lots of things, but no parsley. She put her finger on her cheek to think. What she suggested surprised him: 'Surely there's a Paki shop open round here.'

It wasn't said as an insult. Jaz knew of people who said it without realising, because they were so used to talking only to other whites. Then there were others, inarticulate, who said it through lack of polite alternative. And those who didn't care whether it hurt or not. 'Paki?' he repeated, wondering whether she would show any embarrassment.

'Yes. Short for Pakistanis, people from Pakistan.' She was making thumb impressions round the top of the pastry in the pie dish. 'It's in Asia, you know.'

'Ah-a.'

'We British are such lazy good-for-nothings, especially the men – although I'm sure you and Mr Antoniou are exceptions. Never do a day's work unless there's someone behind them with a stick, but extremely good at setting others to the task. And always on strike. Yes, Mr Sharma, I was on a bus in 1976 when all the traffic lights went out. The people at headquarters who switch them from red to green were refusing overtime if I remember rightly.'

She had forgotten the pie and was enjoying her audience. Jaz listened as he would watch a magician, unsure whether the evidence of his senses was true, trying to decide what was real, unreal, and in between.

'And when the binmen struck I was determined to foil them, and set fire to the accumulated rubbish in the four large bins outside our flats. But the fire brigade came using hosepipes and put it out before it had really taken hold, so after that I contented myself with using my shopping trolley to wheel my own rubbish down to the park after dark, where I buried it.'

'Really!'

'Yes. A neighbour was a binman, but I have to say he was

quite charming even so, and he often told me about the objects people leave for them to collect, including dismembered corpses, so it wasn't a job I myself would have enjoyed.' She wheezed after the dramatic effort. 'I hope the Underground won't strike, because you know I would be either locked in or locked out.'

'Oh, you could come here again,' Jaz assured her.

'Still feeling good?' Tony asked. From Elena's he had brought some paper hats to wear at lunch, and more presents: slippers for himself and a book of Greek cookery for Jaz.

'So that's how they see me,' grumbled Jaz, staring at the window. 'The Cook.'

Tony sometimes loathed Jaz when he was sullen and argumentative, but he would never show it. He spent more energy evading the anger than dealing with its causes; and he knew he'd rather be looking down into the hole than stuck at the bottom of it.

'You know that's not true,' he said softly. 'Don't forget Dino was out of work himself for six months.' He risked a hand on Jaz's sleeve – anything more affectionate would have drawn a counter-reaction for sure.

'And you bought me that bloody apron!'

'Because you like Mickey Mouse.' He combed Jaz's hair back with his fingers. 'Fact is, you can cook. I can't. You cooked when you were working.' Only his gentleness had any effect on the anger, and this time it worked.

'I'll call them later to say thanks,' Jaz said.

Dinner was over. Paper hats had been worn and fallen off, wine finished, and the kitchen was in a state of emergency with a ragged and lukewarm bird its centrepiece. The two men sat together on the settee, the old woman looking at them from her armchair, crossing and recrossing her feet out of nervous habit. She hadn't replaced her outdoor hat after lunch, an omission which expressed her feeling of being at home.

'Happy Christmas from me and Jaz,' said Tony as he handed her a parcel. And she gave them each one of the shapes he had seen in her carrier, before opening her own so meticulously that she was able to smooth and fold the whole sheet of wrapping and lay it by her chair, as good as new. They had bought her a thick pair of climber's socks and some new trainers. Tony had made sure the bag came from Emporio Armani even if the presents didn't. She put the socks on straightaway over her red ones, pulled them right up and stretched out her legs proudly.

She had bought, or stolen, a colour book of classic cars for Tony. It was written in an East European language she may have imagined was Greek. For Jaz there was a striking glass paperweight with a spider inside, which really pleased him.

'Put the TV on,' Tony said.

'No, you.' But Tony put his feet up, and Jaz remembered *EastEnders* was about to start. When he stepped over and pressed the button the picture appeared as usual, but only the faintest sound. He crouched in front of the set and slid the volume control up and down, quickly, slowly, even sideways, but with no improvement. Tony joined him, and changed channels a few times. They turned every knob on the set but nothing happened. In a minute, Jaz was swearing under his breath. The sea of frustrations, having found an entrance, rushed in overwhelmingly as it often did. 'Put it down the rubbish chute!' He slapped the top of the set hard, and a second time, and switched off. Inhibited by Miss Massey, he strode to the window and stared out in silence.

She stood, walked across to the set and peered behind it. Then she went to her room, rummaged in the bags for a minute, and returned with a large, yellow-handled screwdriver. 'Obviously the amplifier,' she said, and slowly kneeled down, as if in worship, and began to unscrew the back of the set.

'Do you know what you're doing?' asked Tony, foreseeing a completely broken TV and an electrocuted guest.

'Of course I do. Wally mended them till the day he dropped dead. Now be quiet.'

Jaz continued to stare outside, but it was an act – his fascination was back. 'Shall I unplug?' he asked.

'The first rule of repair for any electrical implement,' she told him sternly, although it was obvious she would have forgotten if he hadn't mentioned it.

Within a quarter of an hour the TV was on again, and although the volume lacked its usual power, Miss Massey pronounced it 'right as rain.' She sat back in her chair, feet crossed, and flicked through the Radio Times with a moistened thumb. On screen the Fowlers were gathered for their Christmas dinner, bathed in pinks and reds. Jaz, who normally objected to anyone opening his or her mouth during *EastEnders*, asked, 'Who was Wally?'

She suddenly looked as if there was a nasty smell in the room. 'Bad-tempered little womaniser with a face like a building site!' she snapped.

Jaz let out a theatrical gasp. 'No!' Tony preferred him not to act like a queen, but ignored it for the sake of Christmas.

'Of course, he didn't get far, being so ugly. Even used to drive the budgie beside herself with his big face against the bars. I often told him his appearance mirrored his evil nature.'

'So you lived together.'

'Oh yes. He and Mother never spoke for years but as soon as she'd gone he moved in claiming his share.'

In the Queen Vic the beer and the hair-dos had a pink tinge.

'He was your brother!' Jaz exclaimed.

'Of course he was. What did you think?' said Tony.

'I wonder.' She recrossed her feet. 'A severe mistake in the hospital was my theory. Mother was convinced she'd given birth to a girl. Anyway, his side-line was repairing televisions, so we always had almost enough of them in the flat to make up one that worked. It was during that time that I learned to lip-read.'

The Fowlers' Christmas dinner had degenerated into a shouting match – white faces were red, red faces choleric. Jaz turned the sound down and Miss Massey supplied the dialogue. They would never know whether it was correct or not, but it was certainly inventive and cast a new light on some of the characters. Shaking with laughter, Tony went to boil the kettle. A minute later Jaz joined him for a hug.

'You're camping it up.' Tony grinned.

'I've got to, to keep up with her,' Jaz protested, widening his eyes like a little boy in a spiral of excitement, who doesn't want to hear. Then he adopted a determinedly adult expression. 'Sorry. I know you don't approve.'

'It's funny up to a point.'

When they returned with two coffees and a tea with three sugars, Miss Massey was wheezing gently, asleep. They woke her for the royal broadcast, but found her unimpressed.

'What on earth could you have against them?' shrieked Jaz, making Tony wince.

Her Majesty had a pink rinse. 'Mr Sharma, haven't you heard? It's fairly common knowledge that half of them are queers.'

Tony smiled to himself.

Miss Massey had gone for a lie-down after tea. Tony had his head in Jaz's lap as they picked at a dwindling bowl of nuts, and Bob Monkhouse chattered enthusiastically to himself in the corner. 'You know what we call some aunties? Mum's sisters? Massi. A term of respect,' Jaz said.

'Massi,' Tony repeated.

'Longer A. Between "a" and "aa".'

Tony practised.

'That's better. I miss the way they tried to run my life.'

'But you hated it at the time.'

Jaz fed him a peanut. 'I can't win.' Then, less sadly, 'I'll call her Massi from now on. She's the Massi who was good to me at Christmas. She won't know what I'm talking about, of course. Seems to think I'm this colour through being brought up in sunny Eastbourne.'

'She has a weakness there,' Tony said. 'I think my book's in Rumanian.'

The three of them played *Cluedo* all evening, and Massi went to bed at ten thirty, wheezing rather more than usual but promising she would be "right as rain" next morning. Tony began clearing the plates and glasses but Jaz looked at his watch and said, 'Christmas Day's as good as over and not one of my family's been in touch.'

Tony continued tidying. 'It would only have upset you if they had.'

'Well, I'd rather be upset for that reason than for this,' Jaz

16

told him forcefully. They sat watching a black and white film, but it wasn't very good, and Tony was afraid to touch Jaz to comfort him in case it provoked a worse temper. So he lit a cigarette and Jaz moved a little further towards the edge of the settee. By the end of the film, Jaz was so angry that he switched off the set and went to bed without speaking. Tony sat and smoked, and wondered as he had done before about leaving. He thought back to the Jaz he had met three years earlier, a graphic designer with an apparently happy family. He himself was sure he would have handled the family better – well, differently. Mr Sharma senior, a widower, needed gentle handling, but got confrontation. It was Tony's belief that the brothers and sisters and uncles and massis had reacted more to Jaz upsetting his father than to the news that he was gay.

And the job – that had been pure bad luck and economic climate. Jaz wasn't to know that the company he had joined in the summer was about to go into receivership. But whatever the elements of fate and personality, the result was very trying. For Tony each day was travel, work, more work, more travel and then humour Jaz. He knew he would never have begun a relationship that promised all this, but he was usually too tired to know how to extricate himself. Maybe tomorrow would be the day he found the motivation to finish it.

He had promised Massi a breakfast tray, and when he took it in her wheezing was much worse. However, she insisted she was fine. 'Right as rain, right as rain,' she repeated, although he thought she looked flushed.

Jaz was wandering about the flat waiting to start an argument, and Tony's gentle approach was really needling him. Tony locked the bathroom door for some breathing space and sat on the toilet till he finished his cigarette. He hated rows. His own parents rowed – they threw quite large objects at the wall, said things they didn't mean in order to win, and then there was an atmosphere that might last days. He remembered clearly one Christmas when he was five or six, after he'd looked forward to it for weeks, they had been at each other like thunder and lightning from Christmas Eve till Boxing Day, largely ignoring him and the other children. In the end the little boy was so disappointed he had begun to cry, and his mum smacked him in exasperation and sent him to bed. He often dreamed about the row there would be if they found out he was gay. He resolved that if Jaz wanted a fight he could go somewhere else and have it.

Massi shuffled into the living room in her new socks and sat panting opposite Jaz at the table. He tried to smile. 'Better this morning?'

'Ever so slightly, Mr Sharma. Only four hundred and sixty-four days till Christmas.'

He hadn't the energy to correct her. 'Look, Massi, my sister rang. My niece isn't well, so I'll probably have to spend some time over there today.'

'I could see there was something the matter. The bigger the family, the more of them there are to upset you, eh?'

At this comment he did manage a momentary smile. Then he stood up; he felt so bad he didn't want to eat, speak, drink or sleep, and he had the notion that if he switched on the TV it wouldn't work. The answer was to walk away from it – that alone would comfort him. It had worked on several occasions recently. He rattled the bathroom door. He knew well why Tony was still in there. 'Tony. A minute.'

Tony had scrubbed under his fingernails and then shaved, because Jaz liked him to be smart. But Jaz didn't even notice. 'I don't want her seeing me like this. I don't want her showing any interest.' He explained what he had told Massi about his niece.

'But it's Christmas.'

'Tell that to my family.'

'What about breakfast?'

Jaz stared at him with real contempt. 'So I'll be hungry too.'

'Look.' Part of Tony wished Jaz would go, and get whatever it was out of his system; another part wanted to relieve his distress, even for a minute. 'Come into the bedroom where she can't hear.' They went inside and closed the door. 'I thought we could have a stroll this afternoon if you want to go out.'

'No, I'm going now, alone.'

'But we could have another good day together.'

Sometimes Tony's gentleness sounded simply pathetic to Jaz. It was like talking to a wet cardboard cut-out. He need some reaction, for God's sake, some animation. He provided it himself by grabbing the spider paperweight from the dressing table and flinging it at the wall, where it left a small indentation and smashed into a hundred fragments.

Tony left the room in silence.

'Haramzadi Christmas!' Jaz shouted, and rammed his hands to the bottoms of his pockets. He had lifted the tension for a few seconds, but suddenly everything was just as horrible as before, only now there was glass in the bed and all over the carpet. He didn't want to go out, but he didn't want to stay in either, so he put on a warm jacket and left.

When he had gone, Tony didn't feel worry or anger as he usually did, just regret. About ten minutes later, with suds up his arms as he washed the pots from yesterday, the thought floated into his head that instead of mumbling about going for walks, he had wanted to say, 'Don't go. I'm sure I can make you better if you stay.' But such simple words were as powerful and dangerous as fire.

At lunchtime Massi's appearance was quite woebegone. She ate very little and conversation was difficult. 'Don't you take anything for it?' asked Tony.

She shook her grey head. 'The last doctor I saw was the one who came to take Wally away,' she whispered.

'It's very lucky you're here when you're not so well. Just imagine if you were on your own at the station.'

'In this case you are quite wrong, Mr Antoniou,' she told him. 'The station is my good friend; it protects me. When I was young I slept down there often. Yes, during the Blitz. All of us did.'

'What, that same station?'

'Of course. Blankets, babies wailing, the couple next to me trying to copulate quietly – I'll never forget them. I returned to that station quite deliberately when I had nowhere else to go. It's deep and warm and silent.' She began to cough.

He suggested she lie down, and helped her into the bedroom. He knew something was wrong but didn't want to admit it. He had a feeling Jaz would be out some time longer, and hoped he wasn't to be called upon to give mouth-to-mouth resuscitation with no moral support. By four in the afternoon there was an air of deathbed around. Massi hadn't said a word since lunch, but had sipped a little water. The curtains were drawn and Tony sat on the edge of the bed clasping her frail hand as she wheezed rhythmically.

'I'm calling the emergency doctor,' he told her.

'Oh, no, Mr Antoniou,' she whimpered. 'They'll take me away to hospital.'

'No, they won't.' He squeezed her hand. 'The doctor will give you something. I'll look after you here, and you'll be right as rain by morning.'

When he had finished using the phone he sat on the settee for five minutes, smoking. He forgot Massi, and wondered where Jaz was, and whether he was cold. Then he went into the bedroom with the dustpan and brush to clear up the glass.

The doctor was a young black woman. She talked to Massi nicely, and gave her some antibiotics and an inhaler. She folded the stethoscope back into her briefcase and gestured to Tony that she wanted a word outside the room. 'You said she's a vagrant?'

'She doesn't sleep out. . . Well, to be honest, I let her sleep indoors where I work – I'm for the chop if it comes out.'

'What's important is how long can she stay here.'

Tony shrugged. 'As long as she needs to.'

'With warmth and rest she should be fine. It's a viral infection complicating her asthma. You should see an improvement in an hour or two. But back on the streets, she'll die.'

'I couldn't stop her leaving if she wanted to.'

'If she decides to leave, call me. I'll stop her.' The doctor grinned. 'Otherwise I'll be back the day after tomorrow. One more thing – while she's here, whoever smokes really mustn't.'

'Oh, that's me.'

'Not in the flat,' she told him, and he realised it was an order rather than a request. 'And I promise you, your house-plants will perk up, too.'

After she left, Tony switched on the TV and lit a cigarette without thinking. He stubbed it out and began nibbling at his fingernails instead. He had one eye on Bob Monkhouse, one ear on Massi's snores, and half his mind on Jaz, who had now been gone over eight hours. It was dark and very chilly outside, and Tony was expecting him home any minute, cold and tired but ready to be in a better mood. They would have a cup of coffee and Tony would relate the day's highlights. Jaz as usual would refuse to say exactly where he'd been, but Tony imagined him on a bench in Victoria Park and then echoing through the foot tunnel to Greenwich. He remembered how much he wanted a cigarette, and was about to fetch himself some Christmas cake to compensate when he heard a step downstairs in the corridor. But it was for next door.

The clock on TV before the news showed six fifteen. As ever on Boxing Day nothing had happened except this year's breathalyser statistics and some mad outdoor swimmers, smiling. The terrorists and politicians were all cosy at home, no longer divided according to obsession or principle, but for just two days split into the people who love Bob Monkhouse and the others who can't stand him. Tony slept uncomfortably on the sofa, expecting at any second to be disturbed by Jaz's key. Eventually he awoke, still alone, with the realisation that this time was significantly different. It was like his slow realisation that Massi was ill; all the evidence had been there for months that his partnership with Jaz was in trouble. Now it was so bad there was no denying it – only in this case he couldn't fetch a doctor.

It was the first time Jaz had been gone long enough for Tony to realise he missed him – it was an actual physical pang somewhere in his belly, reminding him of the possibility that Jaz would never come home. It had completely overtaken Tony's nagging idea that he himself might enjoy another relationship if one were to come along. He smiled when he realised that what he really wanted wasn't a different man, but a different relationship with the same man. He hadn't been frightened of being caught taking Massi her hot chocolate, and the resulting dismissal; he hadn't been frightened during the afternoon when it had crossed his mind he might be watching her die – he was too confident and practical. But now, now certainly he was frightened that Jaz might decide never to come home. After a moment of paralysis, when the skin on his face felt as though there were insects with wet feet on it, he stood up and went to splash cold water in his eyes.

He couldn't find his partner the job he wanted, and certainly couldn't do anything with his family except make matters worse. He remembered what he hadn't said before Jaz left, 'Don't go. I'm sure I can make you better if you stay.' But, simply by believing it, could he compensate for all those things, really make them no longer matter? That sounded to Tony like a commitment far beyond any he'd ever made before. It might wear off in a day or two like a New Year resolution, or maybe it would be a grand promise you flatter yourself by making, even though you know deep down you can't keep it. He couldn't quite trust his own sincerity. What he did know was that if Jaz returned on his own – whether sooner or later – nothing would have changed. So Tony would have to go out and fetch him, and make the commitment with actions not words.

'Massi,' he said, 'I'd like to go out for an hour if you can manage alone.'

'Right as rain,' she replied. 'Just help me to the toilet and back before you go.'

Rain sprinkled his face as he got into the car. The engine didn't much care to have its Bank Holiday interrupted, but he insisted, so after a little effort it started. He lit a much-needed cigarette (whatever Jaz might think) and drove off. There were only a few people about, wrapped up. Empty taxis passed and an almost empty bus. He didn't bother with Victoria Park and ignored the turn under the river towards Greenwich. Some minutes later he parked the car and walked into the brightness of the station. 'Hi, Tony,' shouted the booking clerk. 'How's you-know-who?'

'She asked me to fetch her a magazine,' he said, making for the lift. As it reached the bottom, a train was rumbling away from the southbound platform. Then there was silence. He stepped quickly down the corridor to the cupboard and opened the door. It was dark inside, but he could see a human shape asleep on Massi's bedding. 'Jaz, Jaz.' For once he wasn't scared of Jaz's anger. Jaz stirred and blinked. Tony looked down at him. The action was done, and the words were in his mouth but he couldn't quite say them.

'How did you know I was here?'

He shrugged. 'Massi. She told me it's warm and safe.'

22

'I was coming home in the morning,' said Jaz apologetically. 'I felt so miserable. I've had a horrible day.'

'Me too,' said Tony, and gave him a hug.

'You've shaved,' breathed Jaz. 'I'm glad you came.'

'Of course I came!' Tony tightened the hug. 'Massi's ill; I had to call the doctor. Now there's a ban on me smoking in the flat because it gets on her chest.'

'She'll be with us for weeks. I could see it coming.'

Tony asked, 'Do you mind?' without being afraid of the answer.

'Course not! She's great. But I've tried being lonely and homeless and a bit mad for a day, and I don't like it. I don't want to finish up that way.'

'Come home, then. I'll make sure you don't.' Had he said what he planned to say, made his commitment? Not in so many words, but had it amounted to the same?

They walked to the lift. In the car home they spoke only a few words, because Tony was wondering whether he had said it, and Jaz was wondering how much he had meant it.

BLUE SNOW

Joe Mills

The park was more beautiful than I had ever seen it before. This is not an observation I make in retrospect; I remember thinking it at the time: it's beautiful, Glasgow Green is beautiful today. I had never thought of it as beautiful before. It was always just somewhere else to play, the only place within miles of where I lived with more than ten square feet of grass. We thought of it as slightly exotic. It wasn't *ours* the way the nearby ghost of Templetons carpet factory was ours.

I had only ever been to the Green before with two or three friends. I would never go alone for fear of the vicious and unpredictable Glasgow gangs, or the alcoholic women (whom I feared more than the men) who would terrify me with their purple-veined hands, their smell, and their pale, dirty faces: faces which were either bitter and threatening or (worse) delirious with their anaesthetised world. Today they couldn't harm me. I was with my mother, protected.

The park was so beautiful because it was winter. Everything in sight was either white or silver. Even the litter on the grass was beautiful: half-buried in snow, half-covered in sparkling silver frost like some new brand of confectionery. There is something about snow: everybody recognises its unique powers, if only subliminally. It's white and clean; it's a talking point; when it's here it's there, it's everywhere. It instils a sense of community, of freshness, change and optimism. And protectiveness: between the white blanket and my mother I felt untouchable, exhilarated. I was only fourteen, but I recognised and appreciated beauty as much

24

then as I do now. In fact my senses were more developed than now when repetition of experience has inevitably dulled them. At fourteen I was like a raw nerve, open to pleasure and pain in equal measure. Whenever I think back to that day, to the minutes and hours before my life was to change so suddenly, I wonder: did I have any inkling of what was to come? Did my mother? She knew part of it, yes, but did she suspect at all how the day would end? I still cannot say, although I remember exactly every detail. I have a vivid image of her sitting on the park bench, hands on her lap, eyes focused straight ahead into the distance, a look of grim determination in them. I remember being worried that her expression had not changed in the past forty minutes. I looked at her several times – the way one nervously glances at a statue, willing some movement, however slight, in the features: but there was none. There seemed to be a battle going on in her head: either a rehearsal of what was to come, or a mental replaying of previous battles. I imagined I heard her whisper to herself, but when I turned round, the same stone face stared silently into the distance.

I was loving (for my age), but moody. I was trying to decide whether to comfort or sulk. I had such a sense of *her* responsibility to me. How angry she could make me when she would take me out on those long walks – in any weather – and speak of her problems, telling me how she wished she had peace of mind. Oh, how that phrase can anger me still! I remember how she laughed at me the day I decided to suffer and smoulder in silence no longer and told her that I wished I had peace of mind too. And it was true: her sadness made me as unhappy as she was herself.

Drawing cruel faces in the snow, I quietly turned to stone like her. I could sit just as still, for longer than she could. Eventually she would speak. I wouldn't answer and she would just have to realise that I was sulking, that I wasn't going to be treated like this.

My father had been gone for two years. The strongest image I retained of him was not a memory of the person but a dream of the person: my mother and I on a bus, both silent, staring ahead as now, like zombies; my father at the bus stop, sadly watching us go away for the last time. This

I dreamed before they split up, even before I knew they intended to. Subconsciously, hearing the muted arguments from bed upstairs, I must have realised how incompatible they were. My mother's violent, clumsy, Glasgow sarcasm was never a match for my father's calm London logic. The accent alone defeats the insecure Scot.

'You're so calm and collected – that's why I hate you,' she would lie to him. The man who stood before me now, who appeared so quietly and quickly in the park, was certainly my father. But he had changed. There was a half-formed blond beard which made him look older than I remembered him to be. But he still had the same searching eyes, peering into mine now as always: Did I love him? Did I realise how much I meant to him? Would I try to be as special as he wanted me to be? Would I never forget him? I remember the tears I wept as I awoke from the dream. There were no tears when I read the note he'd left my mother to give me, telling me that he had to return to England, to leave for good – for my sake. I felt betrayed.

'Hello, Sean.' He shook my cold hand and moved on to my mother's cold face. She had obviously been expecting him. Their conversation started, spluttered and stopped like a faulty car engine in the cold. Within ten minutes the engine was red hot, accusation and recrimination firing from both sides, my presence ignored as usual. It was as though I were drowning and they were watching me, arguing about the best way to save me.

'You should have told me,' my mother said.

I sighed loudly: not that one again. Why were they going over ancient ground? 'I wasn't sure myself. You were in such a hurry anyway. You rushed me.' But why wasn't he certain? He had been nineteen when they married. Even at fourteen I knew I was heterosexual. I almost believed I should be gay: my father was; I had got on better with his gay friends than my own straight playmates; I was sensitive, poetic, a dreamer, frail, unathletic, unambitious, and yet . . . straight. I had no erotic feelings for men, only a desire to emulate some of them. Dean, Brando, Bowie – yes, the gay favourites. I even liked July Garland – but not in the way they did.

26

'You said you would stay away for good!' I wondered whether he had told her our secret.

'You forced me into that statement. Why should *you* have him all the time? I deserve to be something in his life.'

'I don't want him to grow up in *your* world.'

But didn't she realise that I wanted another world, that I wasn't content in hers; that even the weekly letters to my father (that she knew nothing of) were not enough for me; that he, with one four-page letter a week had more influence over my life than she had, with all the time in the world, *and* her physical presence? He gave me lists of books to read, films and TV programmes to see, and an outlook on life that made me *want* to be an adult, experiencing the world. To my mother, who had spent the greatest part of her life here, anything outside Scotland was suspicious at best. All she could do was make me frightened of the world; all she had to offer was blind, motherly protection.

'My world? You make it sound like another planet. You've met my friends – you liked them. You have to admit that Sean liked them. Why is it straights always have some image of homosexuals in their minds that no amount of personal experience will obliterate?'

When I was eleven, a year before they split up, my father's lover moved in with us. It was either that or separation then and there – and my mother at that time still loved him enough, still knew him so little, that she believed he could eventually change. I got on so well with Michael. He was the archetypal fussy Glasgow queen: apron round his waist all day, hands on his hips when he was telling me off. That peculiarly Glaswegian "I've seen it all and can cope with anything" camp clearly appealed to my father with his own rather rigid personality, and comparative refinement. 'These English wans dinnae hiv a clue, dae they Sean.' Michael would joke at my father's mystification at some obscure Scottish custom, and we would mystify him even more by continuing the discussion in the thickest slang we could remember – or invent. At eleven I didn't think of him as gay or straight – just Michael, nice to be with, and he made me laugh.

My mother was never jealous of my father's love for Michael. She just didn't take them seriously – after all, she had borne his child; she had nature and the law on her side. She only began to get discontented when she realised that Michael and I got on so well. She hated it when I went out with the two men. I sensed it with my child's instinct (which means I had eyes, ears and a brain – qualities that parents don't seem to attribute to their offspring until adolescence.)

Eventually she began to fight back. I felt so guilty that, even at that age, I had the upper hand: I could see right through her. At first she attempted to use their homosexuality to frighten me: 'Aren't you afraid you'll end up like that? You'll never have any children . . . people will laugh at you.' She tried pathetically to make me five years old again, buying silly games and toys, taking me out for special teas. When this failed, she exploited the only bond we had: our Scottishness. In truth, this was the only area in which I felt closer to her than my father, whose foreign background distanced him from me to a degree he was unaware of. My embarrassment at my heavy accent, and his attempts to correct it, exhibited themselves in cool sulks and a determination to improve: my mother simply raged at his efforts to change me in any way.

In the end she filed for divorce. The laws of the land gladly gave to her the rights that the laws of nature refused to.

I still retain a mental image of that night which I know I shall never lose, like an old Christmas card from a former lover that gets resurrected in spells of loneliness and self-pity. The sun throbbed cold and red, round and solid in the crystal clear sky. The park was in transition: the white and silver was being washed away by a water-colour edge of yellow and orange, as the red circle dropped below the horizon, the snow drifting from white to powder blue.

Father and I went for a walk. I was to be asked what *I* wanted. What new tactic was this? Or did I know: did I sense in the letters – the desperation and determination? Why did I look back so many times at my mother on the park bench? Why do I always avoid sunset in wintertime – that particular shade of blue; that blue which reminds me of the park, the bench, the handbag with yet another note from my father: this time addressed to my mother.

When would she notice it?

Why were we walking so fast?

THE LADY
WITH THE DOG

David Rees

My children don't know me, Matthew said to himself as he stopped the car at a red light; not as I knew my father: the anecdotes about his past – the 36 bus, for instance, drawn by horses. He pictured the scene as Dad had described it – the Vauxhall Bridge Road, the open top deck, the women with wasp waists and bustles, the snow falling. And then the news that King Edward had died; or was that at a different season of the year, not the same memory? He wasn't sure. But there it was in the picture; the old king dead, snow falling, a horse-drawn bus. Whenever he was in that part of London he drove along John Islip Street, past Landseer Buildings: flats let by the Peabody Trust to the deserving poor – Dad was born in one of those flats. In 1903. A pity, he thought, that he didn't know which. And the old fool wasn't even very lovable, he said to himself as the lights changed. He surged forward with the flow of the traffic.

No, they don't know me. I guess I've told them where I was born, but I can't imagine Rod or Graham rushing off for sentimental reasons to Kettering to stare at the outside of a hospital. They never ask me about the war, what it was like to be a child when doodlebugs were inflicting death and destruction. The rationing, the hardships. The occasional moments of humour. And horror. More concerned at twenty and twenty-two with screwing girls. But he liked his sons and they liked him – that was the difference – though he wasn't always pleased with the way either of them lived: yuppy Rod, Something in the City, was preoccupied with high finance (his

29

advice, of course, had often proved useful), and hippy Graham was wandering round Europe playing the flute and juggling with clubs on the streets of Amsterdam, Paris, Rome. How often did Graham have a bath?

It's probably all my fault, he said to himself as he pulled up by the house in Chelsea; it's the way we live. The way we live, the way we live! Depressing. Unsatisfying. The door opened and there to greet him was Neil, his mistress. Not the right word, but how does one refer to a male lover who is officially 'married' to another man and one is married oneself – to a woman? English, for all its ambiguous variations, has no word for such complexity. Five minutes later they were in bed, their clothes scattered over the floor, and Matthew was penetrating this boyish, male body: the supreme pleasure, he said to himself; nothing in life was as good as fucking Neil. Afterwards, when the moments of ecstasy had subsided, came the post-coital tristesse. There was always post-coital tristesse. They were, both of them, experts at that.

This situation had been going on since Neil was twenty-three and Matthew forty-two – eleven years ago. Matthew's wife and Neil's lover had never found out; neither had the least suspicion. It was rarely difficult to arrange – Charlotte, a London Borough Councillor, had committee meetings several times a week ('Though for all I know,' Matthew said, 'she might be doing exactly what I'm doing;' and when Neil queried the "exactly", 'I *assume* with a man.') Neil's lover often travelled abroad in his work; he was at that moment negotiating a contract with an emir in Dubai. He wouldn't be home for at least a week. 'Why don't we go away for a few days?' Neil suggested. 'I can phone in sick, and you – you're a freelance writer; your time's your own: you can tell Charlotte you have to go to Scotland to research some local colour for your next book.' But Matthew thought it could be problematic; he required more notice – there were things in London he needed to do.

Neil sighed and crossed his legs. 'We exist, you and me,' he said. 'That's all. We have no life together. No shared home. Think of the fun of buying our own little house! Decorating it, furnishing it . . . you and me sleeping in the same bed all night, every night! When did we last do that?'

'January.'

'Ten months ago!'

'Why don't you leave him?'

Neil didn't answer: Matthew knew perfectly well why not, for the question had been asked a thousand times. Leslie was Neil's soul-mate, Matthew excitement – 'Oh, yes!' Neil would say, his eyes radiant, 'excitement! Nobody does it better!' But, he always added, he would seriously consider the idea if Matthew left Charlotte; and he said, again, now, 'Why don't *you* leave *her*?'

'I could. The children are grown up and gone; I have no obligations there. My marriage is nice and comfortable, of course . . . but it's not particularly stimulating. We don't make love very often – just enough to prove to each other we still exist. We go our own ways: she to her committees, I into your bed. I want to leave her . . . though it would be a nasty wrench, and she . . . would be devastated.'

'I daresay she would.'

'But only if you want to leave him.'

Neil was silent for a while. 'It's very simple, really,' he said. 'You and I – we just don't trust each other enough.' He got out of bed and stood by the window, naked, staring gloomily into the garden. Falling leaves, the sour smell of chrysanthemums; another year dying. Another year of frustration, of suffocation, joining the heap of all the others; waste, detritus.

'You have a gorgeous body,' Matthew said. 'Just looking at you and I'm erect again.'

'So you won't come to Scotland with me.'

'Get back into bed. You'll catch pneumonia.'

'I often think these days that . . . that it would be the right thing for both of us if we finished it. Made new lives for ourselves! Apart!'

Matthew grabbed hold of him and pulled him onto the bed. Neil didn't resist. His skin was cool and goose-pimply; he shivered (Matthew's kisses, or the cold? Both.) and the taste in his mouth of Matthew's cock was delicious.

The year died, and the winter celebrations as usual did not allow them to see each other (Neil in Chelmsford with his parents; Matthew's mother paying a state visit and Graham

31

home for a couple of weeks before setting off for Venice) but they did manage a couple of discreet phone calls. They met in January, a blizzard outside: the trees like iron, the dead chrysanthemums and sour leaves burned long since, and Neil, once again naked and staring into the garden, thought the one brave snowdrop in bloom was a symbol, not of a new life beginning, but, in its white purity, of death. 'Where the youth pined away with desire,' he quoted, 'And the pale virgin shrouded in snow.'

'Bollocks,' Matthew said, sleepily.

'I'll leave him. Yes, I've made up my mind! I'll leave him!' He paced across the floor, gesticulating with his arms, his eyes alight. 'Yes, yes . . . I will! What do you say to that?' He turned and looked at Matthew, who said nothing – his expression was completely blank. 'I see,' Neil said. The light died. 'Get out!' When Matthew did not move, he yelled, 'Get out! Get out of my life!'

Matthew did as he was told, stumbling absurdly as he pulled on his knickers. 'I'll see you next Wednesday,' he said.

In May they had a week together in Granada. Charlotte thought Matthew was at a writers' conference in Luxembourg (he had received an invitation to this jamboree); Leslie was signing contracts in Sierra Leone. Charlotte was extremely busy, and this had almost caused a last-minute hitch: it was the time of the council elections, and, because of the poll tax, interest rates and so on, the Tories were likely to suffer a severe bashing. There was no chance that she would lose *her* seat (she had had, for years, an unassailable majority), but Matthew felt, in the general air of doom pervading the whole Conservative party, that he should be in London to give his wife moral support. Not that he had any sympathy for her brand of politics; if he bothered to vote, which he usually didn't, he tended to vote Labour. It was Charlotte herself who reassured him that his presence was not needed; 'I shall be all right,' she said. 'We just have to take it on the chin. It wouldn't be the first time . . . You go to Luxembourg. You've been looking forward to this trip for ages.'

What sort of life, he wondered as he stood in a hot, dusty Granada shop waiting to buy some oranges, did the old woman behind the counter lead? This almost stereotypical Spanish hag, dressed in black, her nut-brown skin wizened and lined, her grey hair swept behind her head and fastened in a bun, one of a million identikit Dolores Ibarruris one observed in every plaza and pueblo in Spain; what would she and his wife have in common, and, supposing they could speak the same language, which they could not, what would they speak of? Babies? Cookery? Margaret Thatcher, Felipe González? There would not be so many points of reciprocation as there would be between a Granada sewer rat and a London sewer rat. Ah . . . the rich diversity of human beings! Can one fathom the values of the architects of the Alhambra, the gardeners of El Generalife? Indeed it was possible: it was the values of those who replaced them, the rigid reyes católicos, that were unfathonable.

And Neil's values, his own? Yes, yes; crystal clear – now – for they had finally decided: he was going to leave Charlotte and Neil was going to leave Leslie. They would inform their respective other halves as soon as they got home to London. They would buy a cottage in the country, in Dorset perhaps; they would own a red setter, create a magnificent garden, eat Dorset knobs and Blue Vinny cheese in sleepy pubs, do everything – everything – together, per omnia saecula saeculorum, amen. It was the easiest thing in the world: they had only to want it and it was theirs. And they did, at last, want it.

It had been a superb week: the love-making, the surfacing every morning in each other's arms, the shared pleasures of the monuments – the wonderful symmetry of the Moors' architecture, their fountains and cool courtyards – and sharing the dusty heat of siestas, the snow of Pico Veleta, flowers in the Generalife, bottles of rioja and valdepeñas, the tapas, guzpacho and cordero asado a la mancheca in pavement restaurants; and a mosaic of little memories, each insignificant in itself, together were woven into a complex addition to the fabric of Matthew–and–Neil – a look over a turret, surprise at hearing a stork talk, a laugh as they crossed a street, a kiss on the balcony of their hotel room, the pronunciation of queso, of jerez, of Café de Los Dos Toros, the softness of skin on a peach, an inner thigh.

On the plane home, Matthew, thinking of this richness and trying to cement it all into his mind, said, 'I love you. Till death do me part.' In answer, Neil, uncaring of what strange looks might be thrown in their direction, kissed him passionately on the mouth.

Disaster. It wasn't a bashing the nation inflicted on the Tories; it was complete rejection. Dozens of impregnable Conservative councils went Labour: every ward in Matthew's borough, including the ultimate unthinkable – Charlotte, by a margin of nineteen votes, was booted out. She was devastated. No more committees. What on earth was she going to do with her life?

'I can't tell her *now*,' Matthew said on the phone to Neil. 'At this moment . . . I'm not that callous! In a month or so, maybe . . . I *will*, I promise . . . I haven't changed my mind.'

'Fuck you!' was Neil's reply. 'Get out of my life! *Fuck* you!'

'I'll see you on Wednesday.'

'Fuck you!' Neil said again, and slammed the phone down.

When Matthew arrived on Wednesday Neil wouldn't open the door: there he was, on the other side of the window, gesturing obscenely. 'I'm in the middle of being gang-banged by ten huge negroes!' he yelled. He pulled the curtains shut with a savage, and satisfying, sweep.

Matthew sighed, turned, and drove home. This was out of the ordinary, he said to himself, not letting me in. Was it significant?

It wasn't. A sultry afternoon in July – that kind of weather when one is so sweaty it seems impractical to wear any clothes; when the air is so oppressive, the horizon so ringed with bruised clouds, the atmosphere so tense with distant rumbles of thunder and flashes of lightning, the skin so tingling that more sex, more sex, more sex is all one wants – Matthew and Neil were doing it again so quickly there was not even a pause for post-coital tristesse.

They had imagined such afternoons would be infrequent now with Charlotte at home, time on her hands. But the fates were benevolent. In one of the ultra-Conservative wards an old socialist had stood; nobody believed he would get in, so his age (he was seventy-seven) and his dicky ticker were not important – but elected he had been, and perhaps it was a flush of joy at the success which had eluded him all his life (such was the theory people bandied about) that cracked his heart: twenty-four hours after polling day he dropped down dead on a bus. (He *had* paid his fare, people said.) The voters, alarmed at their temerity in removing every single Conservative at a stroke, put Charlotte back on the Council at the ensuing by-election. *She* was now the opposition, a role she discovered she enjoyed – to everybody's surprise – as much as she had enjoyed ordering minions around when she was in government.

What if this is an illusion, Matthew asked himself as he and Neil lay in each other's arms, panting, too exhausted to speak; what if – for all these years – he and I have created images of one another that, should we ever find the courage to live in that hypothetical cottage, would prove false? Better to continue as we are. It had begun, really, as a kind of game: fed up with his own company – Charlotte was at a meeting, trying to cajole her audience into accepting plans for a new motorway – he had gone into a gay pub. For devilment, or just to see what it was like; not to *do* anything. And Neil, this beautiful boy, had thrown himself at Matthew's middle-aged and passed-it (so he thought at the time) feet. It was immensely flattering, and he had allowed himself to be flattered right up into the beautiful boy's arsehole. It would not be true to say that from then on it had become serious – that was a gradual process – but Neil did seem to fit every requirement of an unfulfilled adolescent longing. Blond, blue-eyed youth. This is no way to live, he said to himself: trapped in *two* unsatisfactory relationships. I'm fifty-three. I've done nothing, I've achieved nothing; reviews of my novels these days are barely polite; I've been a dilettante all my years – in words, in deeds, in bed. What is the point of it? I'm bored! I'm bored beyond endurance!

What I would like at this moment more than anything else in the whole world is to be in Venice with Graham, the two of us stepping out of the boat as it docks at Torcello, and visiting that unbelievable seventh-century church with the Byzantine mosaic on its back wall.

35

'Suppose one of us has the AIDS virus,' Neil said.

This brought Matthew down to earth with a jolt. 'But we haven't,' he answered.

'So we assume. But . . . as with everything in life we don't know it as a proven fact.'

'I've been to bed with two people in the last twelve years. You and Charlotte.'

'Which is also true for me.'

'Really? I wasn't aware that you'd lured Charlotte into an uncontrollable state of torrid lust for your ugly body.'

'No, you moron. I meant that my bed has been occupied only by you and Leslie.'

'In that case,' Matthew said, 'I don't think either of us has anything to worry about.'

'But we can't be sure!' Neil wailed. 'What does Leslie get up to on his trips abroad? Oh, he says he does nothing, never has done anything, but how do we *know*? On some lonely hotel bed in Riyadh . . . or Caracas or Harare . . .'

'If you're really bothered you can take a test.'

'I don't much like the idea of that. Could I – we – cope with its implications?'

'Best do nothing at all, then. It's safer.'

'Safer!' Neil said. 'Fuck you! You're so selfish!'

'I am selfish,' Matthew admitted humbly. And to Neil's surprise. 'I am. And I wish I wasn't.'

They lay on their backs, smoking cigarettes, each thinking of the implications of a positive HIV test: calamitous implications. Charlotte, Leslie . . . But maybe, Matthew said to himself, that is what I require, a volcano of some sort; it would give me purpose, meaning, destroy my complacency.

'You're astonishingly hairy,' Neil said. He stroked Matthew's chest. 'I'd always wanted a man so hairy I couldn't see an inch of his skin, and my dreams came true! Having sex with you is like being impaled by a savage gorilla! Leslie's quite hairless . . . from the navel up. And when he's making love, not at all like a gorilla. Hirsute; that's the word they write in the ads, isn't it? Strange word. Hirsute. I do love you.'

Outside the thunder still growled. The wind collected itself in the bushes and the rain began to drop, great streaks of it splashing the window-glass.

A year after the overthrow of the Ceausescu tyranny Matthew was in Rumania; an international gathering of writers and artists organized by the new government to show that their country had finally come of age, could do these things as efficiently as the nations of the West. He had to give a speech, but that was no problem; he was used to such tasks. It was all undoubtedly interesting: Ceausescu had left enough of Bucharest standing for visitors to admit that much of it was beautiful, that it still deserved its traditional accolade of the Paris of the East; and there were also the old regime's own weird, unfinished monuments – the bizarre palace and the Avenue of the Triumph of Socialism, now occupied, like Landseer Buildings, by the deserving poor – which, only twelve months after the bloody battles that had led to Ceausescu being tried and shot, had an air of already belonging to the past, of being tourist attractions, of having historical, even aesthetic, significance. The food and the booze were superb (forty years of oppression had not cowed the Rumanians into forgetting that their cuisine was one of the most sophisticated in the world) and the people weren't the brutal bandits that Czechs and Hungarians liked to say they were; they were charming, articulate, eager, and helpful. And the men were extremely cute. The trips into the countryside were the high point: the wild life of the Danube delta; Timisoara, the cradle of the Christmas Revolution; Cluj (though no one was absolutely sure which castle was Dracula's.) Such glorious scenery, Matthew said to himself, again and again – so varied: fertile valleys, snow-capped mountains, villages each with a magnificent church, a land-scape more undefiled by the twentieth century than any other in Europe. How Neil would have adored it!

He did not see other aspects of the Ceausescu legacy – the AIDS babies, the towns and rivers choked by industrial pollution. They were not on the itinerary.

Neil had not been able to come. Ten days was impossible to put together – that amount of time off work, and keeping Leslie unsuspicious. And probably, in Matthew's opinion, he didn't really want to come: Rumania? What on earth *for*? So, despite the pleasures of this unusual trip, he was not happy.

37

He couldn't bear to be apart from Neil for so long; had never been able to bear such lengthy separations. As soon as the plane landed in Bucharest he began to list in his mind all the good reasons why he should leave Charlotte, why Neil should leave Leslie. The only point and purpose of being alive was that he and Neil should be a couple. He couldn't sleep properly – a strange bed at his age was always a problem – and in the hours he was awake he thought constantly of Neil, yearned for his touch, listened to him talking and laughing, saw him in the shadows of the room: at the foot of the bed, sitting at the table, staring, as he frequently did after sex, out of the window. We'll do it, he said to himself; we'll finally do it – as soon as I get back home I shall tell him.

He pictured their future, almost as a teenager fantasises about the boy or girl he worships; the thatched cottage, the honeysuckle, the dog, the Dorset hills. On his last night in Bucharest it snowed: it was still snowing hard next morning. It made the city look magical, like a city in a child's fairy tale; pure, pristine, virginal, which is how he felt about himself and Neil – as if their relationship had yet to begin, could only begin *now*. Even the Ceausescus' palace was transformed by the snow. All fairy tales have ogres, he said to himself, and this one had been killed. The old king dead, snow falling, a horse-drawn bus . . . Why did he remember that, here? On the way to the airport he found he was humming a bit of Tchaikovsky, the waltz from *Swan Lake*: very appropriate, he decided; music that was adolescent, virginal.

He rang Neil as soon as he arrived home; poured out in a torrent all his thoughts and feelings. Neil listened in almost total silence. Eventually Matthew asked, 'What's wrong? You haven't said a word.'

'I've something to tell you,' Neil answered. 'Bear with me . . . it's impossibly difficult.'

'I can take it; I'm a big boy now. Getting bigger as I hear your sexy voice.'

The joke, which would normally have elicited a response like 'None bigger – *huge!*' was greeted with more silence. 'It's Leslie,' Neil said at last. 'He told me, while you were away, that he'd had . . . symptoms.'

'Of?'

'He took a test some while back, apparently. He's not just HIV positive . . . he's ill. He has full-blown AIDS.'

'*What!*'

'On some lonely hotel bed in Riyadh . . . Caracas or Harare . . .'

'Christ!'

'Matthew . . . Matthew . . . what on earth are we going to do? You and me? Matthew . . .?'

ADVENTURERS

Peter Robins

Late in the afternoon, thick soup prepared and set at the back of the stove, Anna Johnson goes to her porch. She makes for a broken-backed chair but, before settling, drops a creased brown envelope onto the scrubbed boards, well within reach. Next, just as she did yesterday and the day before, she folds her hands idly in her lap. At last she fixes her gaze beyond the low hedge of copper beech, the tarmacked road and the flat pasture. If it were closer, or her own sight keener, Anna knows she would be able to distinguish clumps of sedge and the low dunes stretching almost to the ocean's edge. Protected by three whitewashed walls she can observe the effects of a late October breeze on the landscape. Although the wind blows familiar sounds about her, Anna's face is not touched by it. Nor does the breeze expose the white roots of her newly-combed hair.

The postboy, freewheeling in a sudden gust, waves as he passes. He no longer expects a nod in recognition so he is not disappointed. Yet he still greets the woman who'd once treated him as an extra son. As a schoolboy, together with Anna's own two, he'd waited for scones from her oven at five o'clock and, while they cooled, he'd drunk from a jug of frothing milk that either George or Eric had brought from the cowshed across the cobbles. Anna does see the postboy. That is, she registers his passing. It occurs to her that very soon she'll not be able to think of him as a lad just left school. He'll be twenty before the year's out. Five years younger than Eric and six years – to the day – younger than George.

40

She becomes aware of discomfort and looks down. Her thumbs are pressed so firmly against each other that they've grown yellow and bloodless. They remind her of her grandmother's hands, and of one particular afternoon. The old woman had sat, upright and silent, at the kitchen table for three hours after Anna's father had been kicked into the soldiers' truck. With a quick expulsion of breath – more like a gasp than a sigh – Anna forces herself to look up. A graceful web of swallows is banking before it veers south. She follows its progress until individual birds are absorbed in a grey mass. Then she drops her eyes once again to the distant haze. She calculates it will be another forty minutes before the sun falls below the horizon in a scream of lilac and scarlet. Since this is her fifty-fifth October, she needs no evening paper to verify dawn, sunset or lighting-up time. When it is dark, she knows there will be just the winking beam. It is the only light from the village strong enough to penetrate the windbreak of trees to her left.

She sits, recalling – as she does each afternoon – something her grandparents had told her when she was a toddler: 'That light over the harbour's an angel's smile to all seafarers.' At night, Anna remembers, her grandfather had set out under it. Every following morning she ran to meet him as his boat chugged easily into the calmer waters. After close on half a century she can still picture that moment as he levelled with the harbour wall: the old fisherman with both arms aloft, a cod writhing in each fist, and tepid sunlight mellowing his roughened skin. The image fades. Anna feels instead a stranger's weathered fingers – a neighbour's – leading her slowly from the quayside. The lighthouse beam had winked just as usual the following evening but the rhythm of the Johnson household was disrupted. With no grandfather and no income from the fish market it was never the same again. Anna's grandmother called it existence rather than living. And the twelve months that followed brought grimmer hardships. While a herd of Friesians moves steadily across the home pasture towards the milking shed where Eric waits, Anna recounts to herself for the umpteenth time the events of another, never-to-be-forgotten October day.

Foreign soldiers ransacked each smallholding and cottage

on the island, demanding in their coarse language those tiny luxuries everyone had stored against the winter. Even the walnuts and eggs that had been pickled, as always, for Christmas, were taken.

Anna can still hear the indignation in her grandmother's voice. 'Anyone'd think the vandals were scared their ration trucks wouldn't make it through the snow we'll be getting soon enough. Damned mainlanders. What about us? Don't they care if we starve?'

Although she drops a hand to swat a fly that's about to settle on the envelope by her feet, Anna's thoughts linger on that winter. As always, they focus on the last day of February. The intervening years have done nothing to ease the pain this memory evokes. Four soldiers. There'd been four, and all of them little more than boys, as her grandmother said at the time. They prised up floorboards and kicked over everything in the cellar. And then they left, taking almost nothing with them except Anna's father. He waved once. There wasn't time for more as they kicked him up into their truck.

And for what? Anna sighs as she murmurs to herself the answer her grandmother had so often given to that question. 'All for a couple of bottles hidden in the loft. Just a drop of something to warm our bones. My son sent to a camp for *that*. Vandals. What had he done? Brewed up a litre from potato peelings, that's what. Used a few scraps that'd have gone to the pigs anyway.'

Both of her men gone, Anna's grandmother concentrated all her energy on the little everyday routines. Whether they'd been put by neighbours or her grandchild, the old woman countered questions on anything other than household tasks with silence. Each day during the month that followed, she stood by the open door at sundown. What she'd said never varied, and to Anna it seemed her grandmother didn't care whether anyone listened. 'One morning, the ice'll melt on that road.'

There'd been the long evenings shared by the old woman and the small girl. As she sits in her porch with wind beginning to strengthen and pluck dry leaves from the beech hedge, Anna recalls those evenings as a time when she was able to forget her hunger and misery. Warm in the vast bed

42

made by her grandfather's grandfather, she'd first listened to old stories of their family. Her grandmother retold them while unpicking fishermen's torn jerseys for the wool. They were tales of forebears who'd lived and died before photography was invented. Yarns about ancestors who'd left from the jetty in autumns when their crops had failed. And there were other tales, too, of brave souls who'd groaned and ached for weeks in ships that had set sail for America and other newly-discovered lands. As she smiles a little at the recollection of those evenings, it occurs to Anna that – if she's one hope for the future – it is to live long enough to pass on the stories to Eric's children. It does depend on Eric having any; she realises that. Not just on him, of course, but on the slim, red-haired infants' teacher to whom he takes flowers and chocolates. Even if they marry and, for the sake of the farm, have children . . . even then, Anna has to accept, they might decide the past is best forgotten. They might tell her to be quiet and turn on the television instead.

'Now George wouldn't have seen it that way.' Unaware that no one is listening, Anna speaks aloud. He'd known them all: every one of the old family anecdotes. Even before he was seven he'd corrected Anna if she so much as omitted one detail. He remembered little things, like the flute a great-great-uncle had packed, or the coat an even more distant aunt had made from blankets for her voyage to Australia. Not just a coat. It had to be bottle green, he'd insisted. Stroking the dog that ambles out onto the porch, stretches itself at her feet and instantly falls asleep, Anna smiles again. It is not just the dog that causes her to do so: more the memory of another afternoon which the creature's appearance conjures up.

Old Rex was a puppy then, bounding away after anything that stirred among the dunes and the sedges. It was a bright, windless afternoon. George trotted barefoot by Anna's side, looking up with a sunburned nose, while urging her to relate stories that were older still: of islanders whose real names had been forgotten, although suitable ones had long since been agreed on by the villagers. She's done so. George – she maintained ever since – absorbed every detail at first hearing. Wasn't he overheard – she reminds herself – repeating to his younger brother, weeks later, the adventures of those men who'd rowed out from the inlet centuries before the harbour was built? Didn't he describe for Eric the journeys those oarsmen had made – four days and as many nights beyond the horizon – in search of copper and tin and dyed linen? George told it all in the very words she'd used to describe how some of the voyagers had brought back treasures and, sometimes, small, dark-haired women. He added, just as she had done, that some never returned alive.

Staring westward, rotating her thumbs in endless circles, Anna Johnson seems to hear her elder son's voice as distinctly as she had years previously. 'And did those bearded sailors have battles with sea-serpents? Did they go hungry? Did they get ill from fevers?' She tries to recall her reply. It must have been something, she's sure, about pioneers needing to expect dangers because the world beyond the skyline was always full of hazards . . . and always would be. Something else from that still not forgotten afternoon recurs to her. Another of George's never-ending questions: 'And those who never came back, were they being punished for daring to explore so far?' Anna laughs as she remembers this. She laughs as loudly as she did when George asked her and she doesn't care now, as she sits by herself, if Eric does come trudging round from the milking shed to stare at her, and scratch his beard, and wonder at her sanity.

It was the phrase *punished for daring* that she'd seized on. No sooner had George said it than she guessed where he'd picked up that idea. From that moment she decided against letting him go so often to Sunday School. Far better, she'd thought at the time, to let him ramble in the fresh air, out in the fields, and practise his flute. There was no way she'd have the word punishment flung from a pulpit at any child of hers.

Anna's lips tighten. Anyone passing close to the porch would notice an unusual spark of anger in her eyes. Eric, however, is attending to the cows, and the postboy is already in his own room three kilometres away. She's thinking of the village priest. 'Old hypocrite in a black nightshirt.' Though she still goes to his church each Sunday morning, Anna never listens to one word of the sermon. The line of miniature galleons that hangs from cords above the congregation interests her far more. And, after the service, her nod to the old fox – as she

44

also terms him – is barely civil. 'Foxy hypocrite!' The words slip unnoticed from her lips as she thinks of an incident in her own quiet sitting room. She calculates that all of twelve years must have passed since she discovered the priest pawing young George's body. One minute wielding punishment over children like a herder's stick, and the next fiddling about with their jeans. Remembering that afternoon, when she'd walked in merely to ask the creature if he'd like coffee, she decides it was his brazen manner that outraged her as much as anything.

She gives a fair imitation of the unctuous priest, though Rex is her only audience, and he barely raises an ear. 'Ah, Mrs Johnson, I was just instructing George about some matters he'll need to know before being confirmed by the bishop.'

She wishes her reply had been quicker but she'd still not change one syllable. 'Were you, Pastor? Just what is there that farmers' sons like my two, or our neighbour's lad, need to be told about the way the world couples and goes on?' The wind begins to stir Anna's hair and she shuffles her chair deeper into the porch. Rex opens an eye, hoping the evening walk might be earlier than usual. Pulling the creased envelope nearer, so that the wind no longer twitches its flap, she is careful not to dislodge the cassettes. Although she has never taken them from their wrappings, let alone played the recordings of concerts given by her elder son, Anna does consider how far she might have been responsible, with her tales of their adventuring family, for George's restlessness. Outlines of the many arguments there were when George left school drift back. 'So what's wrong with that new college they've opened here on the island, eh? Just tell me that.'

Anna remembers her husband's impatient question. And she recalls adding that the journey would take no more than twenty minutes on a motorbike. George's eyes sparkled at the mention of a motorbike but he did not take the bribe. In his light tenor voice he went on insisting that the local music professors were no more than provincial fuddy-duddies. And they both watched – George and herself – as his father hobbled to the kitchen door, pulled on his work boots and muttered something about just not knowing who George took after. It seemed plain to Anna then – as it does now – that George had taken after her side of the family. Unlike Eric, who never could remember anything except how to repair a tractor or tend a cow in calf, George, like her ancestors, was ever ready to explore. He'd never forgotten it had been his great-great-great-uncle who'd packed a flute to remind fellow-passengers of the island they were leaving. Hadn't George carried that same flute, like an heirloom, with him onto the plane, though maybe for a different reason? In George, Anna knows, there was a wish to learn new tunes rather than to repeat those learned in the village schoolroom or the church.

She doesn't need to turn her head and peer through her bedroom window. She can describe for herself – down to each colour and every nameless face – the photographs on her dressing table. She does so again. There's George receiving his university degree but not looking at all like the foxy priest in his black nightshirt. Then there's George, probably in some bar or at a fancy dress party: a crowd of strangers, all laughing, some of them drinking champagne, and two of George's friends kissing him. And the third photograph. That, George had explained, was taken outside a concert hall in a city she'd heard mentioned on television. There is George again – in the centre of things, as usual – surrounded by friends who'd been to hear him play. All of them looked smarter than anyone on the island. All in suits and ties though it wasn't a wedding or a funeral.

Clouds begin to thicken above her. Scanning them, Anna accepts that the good October weather is breaking up. It'll not be a spectacular sunset after all. Not in any way like the evening when she sat so long on the porch with that telephone message clanging and echoing in her head like the passing-bell. It still seems to her that she couldn't have been there more than an hour, though Eric and his intended insisted it was past midnight when they persuaded her to go with them into the kitchen and drink brandy. Anna realises she has come face to face with the questions again. At first, they recurred hourly. Now (she does a rapid calculation), three hundred and sixty days after the telephone call, some still rise unanswered, but only before sunset when she sits alone in the porch.

46

She works through them like a litany: Where could George's common sense have gone? Knowing himself to be sick, why hadn't he come home? The island's airport had been open for three years. Hadn't he himself used it to dash back for his father's funeral? Why was there never a hint of chest trouble in his letters? Why did he distrust the new hospital in the city? The last question troubles Anna most. She watches dry beech leaves blowing among the purple daisies and wonders why her son wished to be nursed by strangers rather than fellow-islanders. She would have reminded him – if there'd ever been the chance – of two of his cousins among the doctors. At least a dozen of the nurses, she would have said, must have been at school with the boys. Once again aware of pain in her thumbs, Anna releases them and blows her nose on the hem of her apron.

She remembers her grandmother once said that, on the island, everyone was part of a great family, like the swallows. George, she has to accept, seemed to have forgotten that. Even the nameless seafarers, in the stories she'd once told him, were carried home by those among whom they'd been reared. It was strangers who'd carried George in. All of them in smart city clothes and wearing black ties. Even the women had worn them. Of the hours that followed, Anna recalls most just how much the visitors talked. Chattered like rooks, their quick voices rasping against her numbness. Black as rooks, too, they'd seemed to her, in their plastic jerkins and trousers. And all of them rattled on about George: sometimes to her, more often to Eric's intended, whispering away to her in corners.

Reliving those hours, as she does each afternoon, Anna wonders increasingly whether she should not have left all the serving of coffee and sandwiches to Eric's girl. Then she, Anna, would have been free to have rapped her knuckles on Grandfather's old table and spoken to them all. She knows now what she should have said. There have been enough opportunities since to perfect it, syllable for syllable. She'd have told them all to stop whispering as if there was some dreadful secret. She'd have pointed out a few facts, mentioning that the sea had taken George's great-grandfather just as it had taken islanders before the church records started. The story of the soldiers who'd taken her own father to a camp

47

wouldn't have been left out. Loss, she'd have told them, was nothing new. There'd always been wars and there'd always been sickness, and always would be. She'd have mentioned that George's own great-great-great-uncle had never reached Australia to play his flute. And she knows how she would have ended. Just as she would have begun: by asking what all the whispering was about.

Anna vents her impatience – and maybe her annoyance with herself at an opportunity not seized – with a sigh. Almost a year later, she can think of only one sensible thing any of the visitors said: 'George put up a magnificent fight, Mrs Johnson.' Although she'd smiled politely at the time, Anna wondered then – as she still does – what else the feather-brained creature expected. The will to endure had been in George's blood. Of course he'd fought the unforeseen, just like all his forebears who'd ventured beyond the skyline. Sometimes, Anna concluded, those who explored the unknown won. Sometimes they did not.

She stretches her shoulders, picks up the envelope and, before stuffing it in her pocket, checks that the cassettes are in the order that George had packed them. As she gets up and tightens the belt of her raincoat Rex, too, stirs, yawns and looks up. Anna pats his head and then, without another glance to the west, sets off along the road that winds beyond the school and the churchyard to the harbour wall.

LOVE AND ONIONS

Phillip McKew

When we'd been together a year and a half, I decided we'd have our first row. Bugger the pre-nuptial agreement (no rows, no scenes, no camp), I planned the row for ten o'clock. On the dot. That would suit Martin. Nice and precise. Provided he could fit it into his busy Saturday morning schedule, of course. Only one space remained vacant, squeezed in between "having a shower" and "cutting the hedge." The slot that had been marked "sex." It gave us three minutes at least.

Arguing wouldn't be easy (Martin preferred to listen to Pink Floyd when we fell out, usually in a darkened room, lips bricked together, face to the wall, headphones cemented to head.) But I hadn't expected it all to be over before it began. Barely had I got to 'It's time we had a few things out' than he was off.

'If you're going to be silly, I'm going out,' he said. Silly! How dare he! I'd only pulled the plug off his stupid stereo. He may have been around the Block of Life a few more times than I had, but that was patronising. Besides, I wanted to jump up and down in a fit of spontaneous rage. I'd rehearsed. But the bastard just walked out the door.

So I tipped his drawer of colour-co-ordinated socks and pants all over the hall and did terrible things to his plants. Begonias. Busy lizzies. The lot. So what if they were sensitive and needed nurturing? Didn't we all? As I pulled off their leaves I imagined them scream. Then I went out to the gym. Exercise always helped when I felt stressed. I'd joined the club a few months ago, just after Martin had left it. Poor soul didn't have time for things like that any more with his sixty-two-hour-a-week, got-to-make-contacts, let's-make-it-lunch-then new job. Shame. If he'd been there I'd have crashed a few weights on his head.

I looked round and nodded at a few regulars. Now what first? Ah yes, the pec deck. Hands on the pads and we're off. I must, I must, improve my bust . . . As I worked on my chest, my mind drifted off. What on earth had happened since we'd moved in together? The last six weeks felt like ten years. Life was a pile of wet socks and toe-nail clippings. Mainly his. I was scared to get into the bed without checking, for fear that I'd puncture my bum.

Yet that was the least of my worries. Every inch of the flat had become a battleground. Every picture I moved he moved back. Scarcely had we carried each other over the threshold than I discovered he'd no sense of taste. And he said that *I* had none either. We'd had an atmosphere in Habitat last week. Choosing a new sofa to replace his mum's tatty old thing. I wanted Miranda in leather. He wanted Sophie in cane. We couldn't agree and I'd stalked out in silence. Tracy in Dralon still sat in the lounge.

Time for another machine. Legs next, I think. You've got to keep a firm behind now, haven't you? Now he's nice over there on the bench press. I never knew lycra could stretch quite so far. . .

Back to the saga of Martin and me: the final straw had been Alan and Geoff. We'd entertained them last night. An intimate soirée for four. The trouble started the day before when we couldn't agree on what to cook. I wanted to give them lasagne (my favourite.) He wanted duck à l'orange. 'Your duck tastes like rubber,' I said.

'Are they my friends or yours?' he replied. He played *Dark Side of the Moon* at full volume until I gave in.

Then came the soirée itself last night. What a yawn! The clock ticked with arthritic fingers. How much can you say about pine louvre doors? Alan and Geoff knew it all. They agreed about everything too. They would. I wondered it they were really the same person split into two. They even ended each other's sentences. I imagined them in bed. It must be like kissing a mirror – you always knew what would come next.

'Why can't we be like that?' Martin said as he scraped my conspicuously large pile of duck left-overs into the bin. Like Alan and Geoff? I paled at the thought. It even seeped into last night's dream. There we were, Martin and I running in slow motion through clouds of dry ice, calling each other "pumpkin" and wearing identical clothes. I'd woken up with a tension headache. I didn't want to end up like Alan and Geoff. On the other hand we couldn't keep fighting in silence. One of us had to speak up. Hence the attempt at the row.

Still, it wasn't going to ruin my day. If Martin stormed off that was his problem. He could do his thing and I would do mine. . . I finished my work-out, showered and changed and went to the club lounge for a drink. A handful of people sat about chatting. No one I recognised. I channel-hopped a few conversations. Nothing interesting. Still you never knew. I sat back and kicked an abandoned sandwich wrapper under the table. An over-turned styrofoam cup dripped spots of coffee onto the carpet as a vending-machine rumbled next to the door.

Then he walked in. My idol. The Brute. Boobs like King Kong and a grip that could crack nuts at Christmas. I'd seen him a few times round the gym. He looked gorgeous today. A regular five-knuckle shuffle (if you'll excuse the expression.) Dark close-cropped hair and prop forward shoulders – straight from the pages of *Zipper*. He bought a coke and sat back in his chair, legs stretched out and hands clasped behind his head. He had a tiny scar on his collar-bone. I wondered if he clipped the hairs on his chest. As he coughed, I glanced up and noticed his laser-blue eyes were locked fully on mine. I turned away quickly and stared at a stain on the table. Why today of all days? When I'd been single they'd never looked back. I couldn't possibly respond. Window shopping's one thing but handling the goods . . . I crossed my legs and counted to ten. Then I gulped down my drink and stared back.

Now how did one cruise? It had been so long I'd forgotten. Ah yes. *Step One – Look Your Best*. My spirits dipped. I must look like death – and not a mirror for miles. Unless . . . I dashed into the gents and looked in the glass. To my horror my mother looked back. Why had I stayed up so late? It was Alan's and Geoff's fault of course. I pinched my cheeks to summon up some colour (it had worked in *Gone with the Wind*), then I checked the rest. Hmmm, not too bad. Thank God I'd worn my 501s! I flicked a comb through my hair and ran back.

Brute looked up as I returned. Eat your heart out, Martin. I decided to move to: *Step Two – Look Available But Cool*. I raised a provocative eyebrow and leaned back in my seat. To my surprise, he smiled and scratched his cheek until his features fell into a grin. I realised my fly was wide open. Ten for available – zero for cool. I drummed my thumbs on my skull as he stood up to leave. Yet he turned at the exit and winked. I kid you not: he winked. If that wasn't a come-on, what was? Time for *Step Three – Move In For The Kill*.

We met on the street about ten seconds later as a hamburger sizzled on a nearby grill, sending ripples of heat through the air. Words didn't seem to be needed. He dangled his keys before me like the sword of Damocles. Five minutes later we were back at his flat.

As soon as we entered the hallway, he took me straight through to the bed. No chit-chat, no coffee, just Bed. Fast worker, I thought. Then he went to the bathroom, rubbing his eye and mumbling to himself as he closed the door. And *that's* when I started to wonder, as I perched on the edge of that queen-size bed, having recovered from the first flush of lust.

After all, it was a bit odd. He hadn't said a word yet. All of my questions received nods or grunts. I'd given up in the end. It worried me a bit. I mean I like the strong and silent type, but for all I knew he might be weird and kinky. A friend of mine had been in a situation just like this a while ago. He'd been tied to the bed and forced to watch Eartha Kitt videos for sixteen hours. Can you imagine? I looked at the bathroom door. What was he doing in there? Why hadn't he spoken? Two minutes later I knew.

I heard a scream and a shatter of glass. I ran to the bathroom and pushed open the door. 'My fucking contact's got stuck down the sink!' were the first words from his lips. I stared at him. Had that girlie voice really come from *his* mouth? He looked up from the basin, one eye bright blue, the other a watery grey. 'That silly bitch put my picture on the top shelf of this!' he continued, pointing to the open bathroom cabinet. Half its contents littered the sink. 'Look what he's done to it!' he said, holding out a splintered photo frame. It was a picture of him in a modelling pose. 'It was my favourite!' he wailed. I noticed the walls were covered in more of the same.

'Who's *he*?' I asked.

He studied me. 'Never mind,' he said. 'Give me five minutes and we'll get back to business.'

I made my excuses and left.

Back at our flat, Martin had started making a meal. As I walked into the kitchen he was chopping onions. A wilted begonia stood on the table. I felt a twinge of guilt.

'I wondered when you'd be back,' he said.

'You've found the plants then,' I replied.

'I've spent the last hour patching them up.'

'I'm sorry.' I looked at the lino.

'I'm making lasagne now,' he went on. Then he started to laugh. I smiled. I hadn't seen the corners of his mouth near his ears for ages. He gave me a hug. 'Sometimes you're such a little wally,' he said. 'Now chop up those onions. I'll be back in a sec.'

As he left I stared at the onions, remembering something my aunt once said when I'd asked how she'd stuck with my uncle so long. 'Love and onions,' she'd said. 'People have layers. Peel off the first and there's more underneath. If you can cope with the first few, you're made.'

Martin came back into the room. 'Close your eyes,' he said.

'Why?' I asked.

He kissed me on the nose. 'It's a surprise. . .'

TRUE COLOURS

Alexander Wakelin

Rob was on his knees, peering along the bottom shelf towards
the turquoises, his chin nearly touching the floor and his head
angled uncomfortably. He was too engrossed in a range of
particularly violent pinks to look up when he felt the draught
as the shop door opened.

'Robert! How goes it?' came from close behind him.

He unravelled with a jerk, and twisted round to meet a
nose a few inches from his own. It took a moment to focus
on the face. At this proximity he had to assemble the persona
piece by piece – the high cheek-bones and fine complexion,
the bouncing black locks, the smart spectacles, and that nose,
rather elegant and expensively powdered. She spoke again
just as he finally made all the pieces fit.

'I saw you down there through the window and couldn't
resist coming to kick you.'

'Hello, Elaine! Actually, I was just looking for some nice ink
– bluey sort of turquoise, I thought – to get that art-work
finished for you. Just the last touches. I'll be dropping it
in tomorrow, definitely. . .' His words came out with nervous haste.

This was his best client, Elaine German from Apollo
Research. Seeing her made him feel guilty immediately.
Even when he was ahead of deadlines, he was unnerved by
failure waiting for him just round the corner. This particular
piece of work was so urgent that he had made an early start;
but now that it was getting more urgent by the hour he was
already taking longer tea-breaks and finding lots of other little

54

jobs to do. That was probably why he had taken half an hour off to go and choose some new inks down at the stationer's.

His client went on: 'That's great, Robert! We want to get it all printed for a show next month. Tomorrow's fine. Just leave your invoice with Wendy at the front desk.' Miss German re-opened the door, the handle of which she had never let go, and was on her way again before Rob remembered the complication. He snatched the door as it sighed after her.

'Oh no! Hang on!' he called, and she stopped. 'Sorry, it'll be Monday if that's all right. Simon and I – I mean my partner and I – we're going to London together tomorrow. It slipped my mind.'

'Business must be booming!' She smiled.

'Yes, it must.' Rob laughed, though he couldn't quite locate the joke.

'You've never mentioned your partner before. I thought you'd always been a one-man outfit until now.' She set off down the street with a determined stride, the immaculate swathe of her open camel-hair coat sweeping oncoming pedestrians out of her way. 'Congratulations!' she called back over her shoulder.

Rob let the door sigh closed again. He wished his free-lance work really was going well enough to expand. Unfortunately, he didn't have a business partner at all. Simon was his lover. He went to the till to pay for his turquoise ink. It was only when he was fifty yards along the pavement that he noticed the bottle in his hand was violent pink.

By half past six, as he was driving westwards, Rob was still replaying the encounter. Simon, the object of his embarrassment this afternoon, would be calmly indifferent to Rob's confusion. He had always lived a life of simple self-reliance. But Rob felt nevertheless that he had let Simon down, and Elaine, by not explaining who Simon really was. He always intended the euphemism "partner" to be helpfully ambiguous, but it had turned into a lie the way Elaine had taken it. He felt a pang of guilt, and remembered how, when he was a child, his mother could detect the slightest hollowness in his voice, and make him burst into tears with one practised look of disapproval.

He and Simon had been together for fifteen months now,

each keeping on a place of his own, but effectively living together at Simon's. Rob had wanted to move in permanently, but Simon had persuaded him to keep his flat – it doubled as his studio, and he needed to be in the centre of town, where all the clients were. Simon's house was a beautifully neglected cottage ten miles out, situated on a wind-blown hillside. It was what the sale particulars had called "requiring some modernisation," which meant it needed a new roof, new floors, complete re-plastering of walls and ceilings, and the arrival of twentieth-century plumbing and electricity. Thank God they had only met after Simon had done most of this, so Rob had mainly had more superficial jobs to do, like sanding down and painting; and painting and sanding down; and painting again a few more times.

How could he sum up their relationship to virtual strangers with one phrase that was less ambiguous than "partner"? "He's my soulmate" sounded accurate. In fact Rob enjoyed admitting it, and he tried quietly voicing a string of expansions and alternatives. "He's my world. He's my sex machine." Abashed at having mentioned sex out loud, he tried a more wholesome version. "He's my sun," and pursuing the logic, "Together we make the colours of the rainbow." He chuckled to himself and pretended to retch. All of these expressions might have made things clear, but people didn't usually have time for that sort of thing, quite understandably. And anyway, what was that old phrase he half-knew from reading *Antony and Cleopatra* at school? True love beggars all description?

He turned sharply up the last stretch of road, and home – as Rob by now thought of it – thrust its crumbling chimneys between the trees. The windows came into view, still pink in their primer coat applied by Rob twelve months ago in his first fervour to become part of Simon's life. He had worked solidly for two weekends.

Perhaps the best way to explain Simon after all would be, "He's the man whose house I sand."

They sat down to eat in the kitchen, the round oak table between them laid with bread and cheese, a bowl of salad, and a plain crystal decanter of ruby red Burgundy. Simon's taste, and his way of making an atmosphere of warm sophistication in this mess of a house, was not the least of the things that Rob loved about him. The creamy kitchen walls and Simon's few fine drawings and prints hanging on them were dappled with summer evening sunlight through the open window.

Simon was handsome. Everybody felt it about him. He was upright and strong, with dark, gently curling hair. At twenty-nine he was only a year older than Rob, but he had an ease about him that Rob would never have, even if he studied Simon for a lifetime. His blue eyes could transfix anyone they chose to recognise, or evade all attempts at penetration, like a veil across his mind.

Robert was saying (not for the first time), 'I hate being dishonest. I hate not being straight with people.'

'Don't start being straight with me,' Simon joked. 'I don't think it would do much for our love life!'

Robert smiled broadly at the thought of being wanted. 'Perhaps I really should tell Elaine German you're my lover.'

The events of the day which so exercised Robert would never have been thought about by Simon. His calm intelligence would never worry about a problem, as Robert did, trying to find all its meanings and implications. He simply seemed to know the answers straightaway or – more often – know that the answers were of no consequence.

Robert's smile faded as he returned to the problem. 'What do you say about me when you're at the office?'

'At the office? I don't really talk about you much. There isn't much opportunity.'

'Oh, great! It's nice to know I'm always on your mind!' Rob pouted. 'Surely you must mention me sometimes?'

'I don't know, Rob. There isn't anyone I'm that close to at work.' He paused. 'I suppose you do come up sometimes – like if I know someone is going to ring me at home. I tell them my lodger might answer.'

Rob looked even more upset now. He felt a stab of indigestion at the bottom of his stomach. 'Do you have to conceal it like that?'

'I'm all for people coming out, if that's what you're getting at – you know that. I came out six years before you dared to stick your head above the parapet. But that's got nothing to

57

do with telling people all about who it is you're living with at the moment. That's none of their business. It's the same when we're out at clubs together. I don't like going round as a couple all the time, so that everybody thinks they know what to expect from you.' Simon stopped; but he seemed to add as a concession, 'It's nobody else's business. I'd much rather keep you to myself.'

'How can you be my lover when I'm only your lodger?' Robert asked.

'As they say, "What's in a name?" We'll be exactly the same whatever you call us, or I call us.'

'I hope so,' said Rob, pressing Simon's leg against his own under the table. 'I want to stay like this.'

'Yes,' said Simon quietly, and stood up. 'You want to help me do the dishes?'

On the train to London, they had arranged to meet up with Helen and Niall: friends of Simon since they were at university, and a right-on couple who wouldn't miss an anti-apartheid march for all the Labour votes in Lancashire. When Simon came back from the buffet car with four coffees Rob was already trying out his problem of words to use in defining their relationship. They had been through the advantages of "lover," "spouse," and "friend," and had ruled out "soul-mate" and "significant other."

Helen was clear. 'I think you're quite right as you are. I always want to say things which show Niall is important to me, but we don't want to define our relationship too far, in case we burst the bubble. That's why we won't get married. It puts a kind of public pressure on a relationship.'

'Remember Mark and Sarah from college?' said Simon as he squeezed back into his seat.

'That's right! They were wonderful together for three years, and just about the day after the wedding Sarah started thinking she knew how to sort Mark's life out for him,' said Helen, staring at the dried brown dribbles down her plastic cup. 'So we just say "partner," don't we, Niall?'

'The trouble is people usually just give me a blank look when I say "partner" – as if they haven't got the foggiest what I'm talking about. I usually call you my wife, to be honest. It's

lot less hassle. And then of course I don't want other men
thinking they can take liberties with you!'

Helen glared.

Robert came to the rescue. 'There's an old queen in our
village who has a toy boy at least fifteen years younger
living with him, doesn't he, Simon? He goes round the village
talking about his cousin.'

'Yeah. Nephew would be more believable,' said Simon.

Robert laughed. 'Either way, it's a bit dodgy. I'm sure half
the neighbours have rumbled their relationship by now . . .
and the other half think it's incest!'

'That's so sad!' said Helen. 'They can't really mean much to
one another. Do you think they just pretend to people, or are
they pretending to each other as well?'

Simon was looking out across the flat fields. 'If it gives them
a kick. Everybody sees things the way they want to.'

As the train pulled back into countryside after the next
station an elderly woman was banging her way down the
gangway, struggling with her luggage. Simon leaped up to
help and lifted her two carpet bags and a crocodile hold-all
onto the rack opposite. She was full of thanks when she
had settled. She burbled on happily from her seat across
the gangway. 'I do love train journeys, don't you? I meet
such interesting people. I'm Rose, by the way.'

Helen giggled, and introduced herself. She smiled significantly at Rob, then at Niall, and said, 'And this is my
fiancé, Niall.'

'Oh, how lovely! Have you set the day?'

'Actually, no. We're not thinking about that just now.'

'Well, never mind, dear. I think you make a lovely couple.
Wonderful to see two people so happy together.'

Looking for more names, the woman turned to Simon
expectantly, but Robert saw his chance.

'I'm Robert Jackson,' he said in his politest voice, 'and this
is my boyfriend Simon.'

'How quaint,' said Rose. 'One doesn't hear that word used
by boys about one another these days, in case it's misin-
terpreted, I suppose.' She laughed. 'Although my daughter
Alison always had lots of lovely girlfriends of course! Isn't
that funny?'

Helen and Niall held their breath. Simon laughed mechanically with the woman, trying to deflect Rob's gesture. But Rob persisted. 'Well, in this case he really is my boyfriend, and I love him dearly.' He smiled, as winningly as he possibly could.

After a few moments, talk across the gangway quietened, and the four friends attempted to revive their own conversation. It seemed only minutes later that they arrived at the woman's station and she was up again, politely bidding them all farewell, and stumbling off down the carriage.

An hour later, at Euston, all four tried not to see the woman's crocodile hold-all and carpet bags being lifted off the train, two carriages further down.

At the march Rob and Simon had some time away from Helen and Niall at last, amid the shifting mass of banners and straining voices.

'Why did you have to embarrass me like that on the train? It was appalling,' said Simon, staring straight on into the marchers ahead of them while Robert looked at him in amazement. 'I don't see why you have to make such an issue out of saying what I am to you – whether I'm your friend or your lover, or your fucking lifetime partner.'

Robert could feel that if he tried to answer his voice would be tight and high, and he waited a moment before he said anything. 'I suppose I want to tell people how important to me you are, that's all. And I don't see why we shouldn't be just like any other couple who say they are together – and be treated like Niall and Helen.'

Simon's anger made him quick. 'What the hell does "together" mean? All four of us were "together" on the train. We're all "together" on this march, aren't we?'

'Come on, Simon. You know what I mean.'

'Yes, I know what you mean, but maybe it's not what *I* mean, and maybe all these people here think something different. Look, if you want to tell complete strangers about yourself, you go ahead. But don't *ever* make it all about me. O.K.?'

'But it *is* all about you, Simon!' Rob couldn't compose his reply this time. He felt the heat of emotions he wasn't used to, burning at the back of his eyes. '*You're* the thing I really want to tell people about.'

The shouting got louder as the crowd passed a cordon of mounted police, and it was hopeless trying any longer to explain. They were pulled on into the crowd and gradually separated by the bodies moving between them. It seemed as if Simon were being sucked always to the further side of people next to him. As time passed, Robert could only just see him, over the heads of the crowd, laughing and shouting with another marcher, far away and ahead. It seemed as if hours passed before they were close again.

At nine thirty on Monday Rob took himself to the front entrance of Apollo Research. It was big: post-modern furnishings, mahogany and glass doors which opened automatically when you approached, and a long glass bay filled with a luxuriance of living plants. Rob was always pleased when he saw real plants (of variable shapes and colours) in his clients' offices. He walked up to reception with his art-work clutched close.

'Hello, Mr Jackson. Got some more pretty leaflets for us?' asked the receptionist. He never could work out how she should be able to remember his name. 'Have you brought your invoice?'

'Hello, Wendy.' Her name came to him effortlessly. He handed her his bill and hoped she wouldn't see how small it was. 'I've got the art-work here, but I'd like to go in and have two minutes with Elaine German. Any chance?'

'Germy? She's not too busy today. I don't think she'll mind if you pop straight in. You won't be more than five?'

'No, sure. Wouldn't keep a busy woman.'

He went to the stained beech door marked *Dr Elaine German, Manager, Corporate Client Relations*. He never knew she was a doctor; and it didn't help. He knocked lightly and leaned down to the keyhole. (He hated not being sure whether he'd been called in.) He waited a moment. Was he being ignored, or couldn't she hear him? He decided to knock more assertively. The door lurched open. 'Yes! Bloody come in, I said!' She was gone again back through the door before he could do anything except look stunned. He recovered himself and followed her in.

'Ah. Elaine. There was a bit of a misunderstanding. . .' He stopped, having realised she was on the phone. He stood in front of her desk, feeling as he did when he was seven and had the biggest telling-off of his life, for playing a sort of touch with other boys at school, chasing round the playground pulling down each other's shorts.

'Right then, George, we'll call it fifteen thousand for this month, then. O.K. Great speaking to you.'

She put down the phone.

'Yes,' she said.

'Well, I. . .' He hesitated. 'Was it pink or turquoise you wanted for the background?'

'I don't remember us discussing that, did we, Robert?' She looked dangerous. 'You have finished it, haven't you? We really need it today.'

'Ah yes, here.' He pulled the design folder out of its huge manilla envelope and slid it onto her desk.

She didn't even pull back the protective tracing paper before exclaiming, 'Hell! That's . . . er . . . pink!' This was the first time Rob had ever seen her lost for words.

'Look, if you don't like it I can re-do it. Have it done by this afternoon.'

'No. I think it'll grow on me. It's certainly striking, which is what it needs to be.'

'If you're sure you're happy. . .'

'Yes, it's fine.' She put the art-work to one side. 'Did you give Wendy your invoice?'

'Certainly did.'

'Great. Lovely to see you, Robert.' She reached across the desk and shook his hand, but he didn't turn away. She looked surprised. 'Sorry, was there something else?'

'Yes, nothing important really,' Rob said, gradually gaining confidence. 'It's just when we met the other day.'

'Thursday, yes,' said the doctor, hurrying things along.

'I said I'd got a partner . . . or at least you thought I said I'd got a partner . . . well I did say that actually. . .' The doctor was looking increasingly ready for her next appointment. He hurried. 'What I mean is, I don't have a business partner. I just happened to mention that I was going to London with Simon. But he's my spouse, my lover. . .' He continued more quietly, and almost to himself now, 'We've been together for a while.' Once again, she seemed lost for words, so he filled the space. 'Not my business partner.'

More silence. Then suddenly, 'It's not really any business of mine, is it?' she said, with at least as much hostility as in his worst imaginings. 'You can do what you like in your private life. I don't want to know about people's private lives.'

Silence again.

'Right.' He was getting angry now. He wasn't making a big effort to tell the truth just so as to be abused. 'I didn't want to leave the misunderstanding in the air.' He tried a joke. 'I couldn't have had you thinking business was booming. You might have tried negotiating a better price or something.'

He wasn't quite sure now what her reaction was. She looked out of the window for a moment, then turned to him. She spoke rather softly. 'Well, I may work in a bigger company than you, but I have a partner too – a long-time one.' Her smile gradually broke. It was a more credible smile than any she'd shown him before – in her professional capacity.

'Ah!' He hesitated. He opened his mouth, closed it, let its edges turn up with an inexorable tightening of his cheeks, and burst into a silent beam.

She hesitated, staring him straight in the face, then moved on. 'Look, we've got a big job coming up. A whole corporate image for the company. I'd really like you to do it, but you might have to expand a bit.' She smiled. 'Take on a partner, that sort of thing. . .'

In the afternoon Rob went back to the cottage and packed some belongings. He left a note on the old table in the kitchen:

Dear Simon,

I'm not here. I think I can see now that perhaps we want different things. I could go on hoping, but maybe it wouldn't change how you feel. Not seeing each other for a bit will make it all clearer.

Look after yourself.

All my love, always,

R.

FILIPINO STING

Michael Wilcox

Gay Scotland magazine, personal ads, spring 1985.

> PHILIPPINES: Good looking guy, 22 years, 170 cm tall, oriental, gentle nature, funny humour, seeks mature man for sincere, honest, gay relationship. Interests: travel, cinema, theatre, literature, music, gardening, expert Asian cook. Well-hung body, sexually imaginative. Psycology student. Write Francisco Angelo, Bacolod City . . . etc . . .

Rannoch
Scotland
3rd April 1985

Dear Francisco,

I have just seen your advertisement in *Gay Scotland* and have decided to write to you at once. This is the first time I've answered such an announcement and I'm not sure how to go about it, but here goes.

I'd better tell you honestly from the outset that I'm fifty-seven years old (young?) and have retired from industry. For more than twenty-five years I worked in the woollen trade (you've heard of Shetland wool?) and I'm sending you a gift of a sweater made entirely from Scottish wool by separate post. To get the right size, I measured out 170cm on the living room floor (in front of a blazing log fire) and lay beside it to see how tall you were in relation to myself. I then figured that at twenty-two you'd be slim (lithe? athletic?) and reckon that the one I've sent you should fit you. Let me know if it doesn't!

I live alone near Loch Rannoch. A loch is a large lake and Loch Rannoch is many miles long. There are forests and wild moorlands and mountains nearby. From my beautiful garden, I can see the rugged peak of Schichallion, a magnificent mountain of more than three thousand five hundred feet. I also like going to the theatre and each year I take out a subscription to the theatre in Pitlochry. I have a car, of course, and Edinburgh is about two hours away (Edinburgh is Scotland's capital city) and there are concerts and opera there. I often stop overnight in Edinburgh, so you can see I have a really good time.

The thing is that most of the time, I'm having all this fun on my own. I am gay, or homosexual as I prefer to say, but I'm quite shy about it. I don't like to go to nightclubs (all that noise and cigarette smoke!) and although I go occasionally to the Commonwealth Baths (the sauna mostly) in Edinburgh, I'm *very* cautious about speaking to anyone. So it must seem odd that I'm writing to someone I've never met, who lives on the other side of the world, hoping that he will respond to my letter.

I imagine that you'll get hundreds of letters and the idea of forming some sort of relationship with an old fellow like me . . . a lively old fellow, mark you . . . won't appeal much to a young man in the prime of his youth. Anyway, I hope the sweater comes in handy, and I would so much like to have a letter from you.

Yours sincerely
David (McNee)

P.S. They spelt 'psychology' wrong in the ad!!

Bacolod City
5th May 1985

Dear David,

Hie there! I receive your "sweater!" It's so warm. So soft. It prickles my skin when I wear it with nothing else on. Can you imagine me with just your "sweater"? I am very happy to have it, David. Oh thank you, my dear, my Sweety. That's what you are to me. I call you Sweety from now on because you love me so much!

I enclose some photo. That's me! I know it's naughty, but I thought you want to see what I really look like, how well- hung I am. It's true. You can see now. Oh Sweety, how I long for you. I am expert at Asian massage and receive many compliments for what I do. I relax you and I excite you and you are my man, my plaything, my lord and I love you. Very good at Asian cooking to. I cook for you one day when we meet and we play by your log fire. That would be fun, Sweety, and we make ourselves very happy. That's what you want isn't it. That's why you write to me.

Now let me tell you about myself. I am still a student that's the truth. I am studying psychology (good speller) but I have nearly finished now. My family no longer look after me I look after me all time. I have many brothers and sisters and my mother looks after them now. I am success I am student and my family are very proud. But I love to have an older man so you at fifty-seven are ideal man for your Francisco perfect gift from Heaven for me. I have to make money for my studies so I do modelling, very sexy body, when I can do it and I do massage for tourists but I'm very careful with Americans and keep my body clean and fit and I'm very healthy you know what I mean, Sweety. So when I graduate this summer I want to travel and that's where I hope you can help me. How I want to visit you and see your mountains and forests and moors all wild! How you could show me Edinburgh and the opera and the Commonwealth Baths! Oh Sweety we have so much love together so happy and our souls unite in pure bliss from Heaven.

Oh Sweety do write me again and forgive my wicked photo but I thought you'd love it and do send me many international reply coupons so I can write to you and send more photo would you like really naughty ones?

Love love love my arms are around you as I sleep.

Forever bliss,
your Francisco

Rannoch
20th May 1985

Dear Francisco,
Your letter and your extraordinary photograph have just arrived. I am very happy to hear from you. I think your photo is splendid, although I did wonder who took it. I enclose a photograph of myself (recent) but as you can see I am not

naked or lying erect on an animal skin. Instead, I am in my garden and you can see Schichallion in the background, which, I suppose, you could describe as a magnificently rampant mountain.

I was most interested to read about your family and the ways that you are trying to make ends meet. Do you have any photos of yourself modelling? I'd be most interested to see them if you have. I'm fascinated to see any photos that you have, so there is no need to be feel shy about what you send me. Although we Scots are brought up in the stern shadow of the Kirk (our puritanical religious background) this seems to make us all the more mischievous when it comes to matters of the flesh. I believe that fresh air, a high fibre diet and the Kirk are primarily responsible for the extreme randiness of the Scottish male. I have a great deal of the first two (less of the third now) and it certainly creates a desperate need which is not easily satisfied in these parts.

You must, of course, complete your studies. But I gather that you will graduate this summer. Are you planning on travelling when you have finished? If you find your way this far, I would be delighted to meet you and show you around. I have plenty of free time on my hands and would love to introduce you to the delights of Highland hospitality. I am not a spectacularly wealthy man, and I should make it clear to you now that it would be quite impossible for me to fly you over here from the Philippines, but if you were able to travel this far by your own means, it would give me great pleasure to look after you for a while. I mean until you've had enough of me!

I went down to the post office at Kinloch Rannoch and bought them out of international reply coupons (more are on order) and I enclose enough for you to be getting on with. Looking forward to hearing from you soon, and seeing more photos.

Love,
David

Bacolod City
22nd June 1985

Dearest Sweety,
Hie from your lover! So much has happened so busy! I've

been working in Manila modelling! Yes it's true! I met this man and he engaged me and paid for my trip to Manila and the hotel (very luxury!) and I had to model sport wear shorts and tops and shoes very fashionable I looked ravishing. You would have been very creamy if you had seen me I tell you! I behave very well and keep your photo by my bed at night and I look at it and I love it very much. I talk to it and say dearest Sweety my David how I love you and I have all this good fortune since I receive your letters and you must be my guardian my angel you see I am Angelo to and we are united as angels in the highest. And I never let this man touch me though he try to many times very naughtily but I smile and tell him I am given to my lover and it is you Sweety! You are my lover now and you make my life sunshine and show me Heaven. I long for your caress and know that you will take me in your arms when you see me and how gentle I'll be with you and do your service.

And now I am back in Bacolod City in my room (with the animal skin) and I lie naked as I write to you and under me is your prickly "sweater" which I love and keep as my secret gift and it excites me a lot! It smells sexy Scottish wool have you noticed? Oh I am hot hot hot my lover. And I'm reading many books for my studying and in the library I look up on the map where Scotland is and it's very far like another planet. And I've found Edinburgh, Glasgow and Dundee but I cannot find your erect mountain I'll keep looking.

I have wonderful news! My uncle who lives in Amsterdam he runs a shop selling Asian art works he came to visit my family and he has asked me to visit him after I've finished my exams next month. He is paying my air fare to Amsterdam and I went to K.L.M. today and got my ticket! I shall be near you dearest one, and surely you shall meet oh wonderful wonderful. But all I need is for you to help me oh please help me, Sweety, with the fare from Amsterdam to Edinburgh (or should I fly to Glasgow, or where should I fly?) If only you will pay for the ticket we can be together. I asked at K.L.M. how much it would be from Amsterdam to Scotland and it would only be about three hundred pounds oh do not desert me now in my hour of need. My bank account number at the National Philippine Bank, Bacolod City Branch, is 8574239532 and all you have to do is send a cheque made out to me with my bank number and send it to my bank and they will cash it for me and I can buy the ticket. Oh do not be angry with me please help me now there is no one else can help me but you. We will be only an hour apart, my Sweety.

Oh I cannot bear to lie here without my love. If only I could leave tomorrow but I cannot. Exams exams help! I will send my soul flying to you and you will take me in your dreams and I will comfort you with my embrace.

love for evermore
Francisco
and!! P.S. another photo am I too bad for you?

Rannoch
10th July

Dear Francisco,

Thank you for your letter and for the new photo. No, you're not "too bad" for me yet, although you're one of nature's fallen cherubs without a doubt. What you are doing could be unhygienic if you fail to wash your hands afterwards (which I'm sure you do!) I must admit that I'm excited by the prospect of your visit to Amsterdam. After some thought, I decided to check out the prices of air fares from Amsterdam to Edinburgh Airport (that's the one you want.) And I found out that it doesn't cost anything like three hundred pounds. It may cost that if you try and buy your ticket over there, but if you wait till you get to Amsterdam and but a cut-price shuttle ticket, you can get a return to Edinburgh for less than one hundred pounds. So . . . dear Francisco, I have visited my building society and arranged through them to send you exactly one hundred pounds, paid into your bank account (how wise to have things so organised!) All you have to do is wait till you get to Amsterdam, then phone me and tell me when you're arriving at Edinburgh and I'll drive over and meet the flight. One hundred pounds is more than you'll need, so you'll have a little extra pocket money as well.

Your letters have had an interesting effect on my life. You sound so vivid. I love your sense of excitement. You give me a great deal to live up to and I'm worried that your expectations of me will not be fully met. I do promise to do my very best to give you a wonderful time while you're over here. I will treat you well and make you a very special person in my life. I've been walking on air since you started writing to me. My life suddenly seems worth so much more. I'm deeply grateful to you and although we haven't ever met I really feel a lot of love for you. There is so much here that I think you'll enjoy. We can tour around the Highlands and do some mountain walking. I'll take you to Edinburgh. Soon there's the Edinburgh Festival and the city fills up with artists from all over the world. There are some wonderful concerts at the Usher Hall that I'd love to take you to. I think you'll be amazed! I haven't told any of my friends about you, but I will now. We'll organise splendid dinner parties in your honour! Traditional Scottish cuisine (plenty of red meat to make your blood boil!) And I'll buy tickets for the Festival firework display. It's a great event with exploding rockets lighting up the castle.

Please write to me as soon as the money gets paid into your account. My dear Francisco, we shall be so happy together. I enclose some more international reply coupons. At the post office they're wondering what on earth I'm doing with them all. Tongues are starting to wag but I don't care any more. I'm so happy. Write soon and keep sending the photographs.

Love
David

P.S. I'm sending you some woollen gloves and a scarf (Scottish of course) for the journey.

Bacolod City
6th August 1985

Hie Sweetypie,

Terrible news! They've changed the dates of my exams so that I've had to alter the dates for my trip to Amsterdam. Why do they do this it's so unfair. I am very unhappy boy not to be travelling. And I have your money that you sent but it isn't really enough but it is kind of you to send me some.

I am very bitter with the exams that I am a prisoner here with my studies and cannot come to you my lover. You know I must do exams I must stay. No more modelling yet but I hope they will. Oh I am in despair. Why don't you fly here and I can show you how beautiful it is. We have Very Erect mountains very exciting ones and wild and dangerous with bandits even! I can show you my family and they will greet you as friend and make many presents to you.

My handwriting is very funny now because I write with your wool sex gloves and the pen slips. Scarf and gloves and sweater are too hot to wear out in the sun so I wear them in my room and my friend will will take a photo of me wearing just Scottish wool how jealous my friends are and I touch them with my sex gloves and they squeal! We all have a lot of laughter about it and it is thanks to you that we are so funny.

I don't know when I'll fly. I lose all my money for the ticket not being used. Despair and unhappiness for ever. Oh rescue me my friend. I am weak with weary study. My friend photos me and I sleep then.

Short letter but full of love for my dear one.

Francisco

Rannoch
1st Septermber 1985

Dear Francisco,

How sad that you aren't here. I was looking forward to your visit so much. The Edinburgh Festival is in full swing and I'm writing to you from my hotel room, although I've put my home address at the top of the letter so as not to confuse you

However, what has saddened me more is that I was talking to some friends in The Laughing Duck (that's a gay bar) and they have told me that quite a number of other people have been in touch with you. I gather that you have been writing to them in much the same way as you have been writing to me. Then someone produced a photograph (which I hadn't seen before!) of you in a most provocative posture on your animal skin wearing only *my* sweater, *my* scarf and *my* gloves! Then, to make matters even worse, I see in the latest edition of *Gay Scotland* that your original advertisement has re-appeared, complete with photograph this time! Are you completely shameless? Am I wrong in thinking that you are simply part of a racket to trick people out of money? All those things you said to me, you've said time and again to others.

What a fool I've been! God knows I'm old enough to know

71

there are swindlers in the world. But I wanted so much to believe in you. Please write and tell me I've misunderstood everything.

Sad and disillusioned,
David

Rannoch
10th November 1985

Dear Francisco,

One last note, since you haven't even acknowledged my last letter.

You have been on of my mind all these months. I've found out that quite a number of people have been tricked into sending you money. Had it occurred to you that for a few hundred pounds you might have thrown up the chance of something special happening in your life? I think you would have found me kind and generous. There are many things that might have been which you have sacrificed for a paltry sum of money. Are you sure you backed the right horse?

I've been busy today sawing logs and splitting them with my axe, getting ready for the winter months. It has been a breathtakingly beautiful day, with the first snows upon the mountain-tops and the autumn colours brilliant in the cold sunshine. I was alone. I was happy to be alone. Then I thought I heard someone whispering and I turned round. A feral cat had crept out of the Black Wood and was eyeing me with mistrust. I spoke to it softly. I welcomed it. It sensed that I wasn't a danger and trotted across my yard to continue with its hunting. I'm part of its wild world. It'll steal my hens if it can. I have a gun. I won't shoot it. We understand each other.

Goodbye,
David

THE OFFICE BOY

Paul Mann

I think of Boyd, with his wild dark hair and deep blue eyes in a pale face, as black Irish. The initial impression yesterday was one of a trouble-maker, one who hangs about street corners in a leather jacket. He's too cocksure, too knowledgeable about motorcycles – he doesn't own one – and he knows all about soccer, and this morning as the watch expert he took apart his watch. During the day and a half he has sat next to me in the office, he has helped himself to pens and stationery from my drawer: it is as if instinctively he knows I don't mind. He has sung, drummed his fingers and sworn several times. The child in him showed when he was told off by Hannah, for then his face had no expression; the rebuke appeared not to register. Yet yesterday evening, when I was sarcastic and said I would be glad when he went home so I could have some peace, there was sudden hurt in his eyes and he asked sincerely: 'I'm not that bad, am I?'

Boyd has chosen me to be his friend.

Valerie sits at our table and is disliked. 'Look!' she says. 'He can't walk in those boots. If he had any bum at all it would wobble.'

Hannah opposite peers over the top of her spectacles. 'He's a boy still. Growing into a man. Why, he's really quite beautiful.'

He returns to his seat. Now he is effervescent; we are to play a game he explains to me. We are to run through the alphabet choosing a dirty word for each letter. I start with A for anus and he follows with a sedate buttocks. We reach F and he is

73

in silent hysterics; he jumps up, holds his stomach and Valerie is seething, the hate showing in her face. Gobble is acceptable and we negotiate knickers and he is obviously prepared with nipples. But the W is quite a hurdle: he is cracking up; he leans forwards towards me so Hannah can't hear and mutters, 'Wanking.' He is going out of control.

'You're too loud, Boyd. Shut it!'

Instantly he quietens and as it is his break he reads my newspaper. 'M.A.S.H. tonight. It's one of my favourite programmes.'

'Glad to hear it.'

'It's liberal.' He smiles. The sloping back teeth show; he moves his head proudly; his mouth stays open, his eyes fixed on mine. He knows I like him. He reaches out with his hand and rests it on my sleeve.

It is easier to concentrate on my work after Boyd leaves, so I stay late. It is quiet in the office and few people are around. Peter comes in to file. Peter is seventeen and is distanced by his shyness: he never talks of sex or drink; there is a girlfriend he speaks of when asked.

'You been away, Peter?'

'I've had the flu.'

'You still look a little flushed.'

He is pleased at my concern. He is an extraordinarily handsome young man. He wears red shoes and pants of a different shade of red and a darker red shirt. All this fits; all these clashes of red are marvellously just right. Black, heliotrope, orange or any goddam colour would be just right on Peter. He would be dignified naked, in fact quite beautiful naked, although perhaps one would see the Michelangelo figure, not sex. He looks at me as Boyd does in the eyes, but Boyd has much better eyes.

Boyd is irritating this morning, insisting on doing the crossword puzzle during working hours and is impatient when he cannot find the answer to a clue. I overhear him boasting to Hannah that he drinks at least three pints each lunchtime. It is almost one o'clock, so I zip up my anorak and casually ask, 'You coming for a drink?'

Not hesitating, he answers: 'Yeah.'

The King's Head is drab thirties; there are a handful of locals left from before the present landlord took over and they sit stoically at their table and talk, seemingly oblivious to the camp old thing behind the bar, the gay magazines sign and the various men who drop in.

'I haven't been in here before,' says Boyd.

'It's gay. Does that bother you?'

He glances sharply about the room, and, thinking, he picks up his glass of lager with blackcurrant and asks: 'Is it queer?'

'I've just explained.'

'It *is* and I'm here! *Kinell!*' I don't think he's noticed the couple by the door. He sees me looking at them, and now he studies them, listening to shrill voices. 'Are they?' he hisses.

'What?'

'Queers.'

'No – they might be homosexuals.'

'I said that. That's what I said.'

'I'll get you another drink.'

He shakes his head. 'I'll buy you one. You can have a double whisky if you want.' He thinks, then adds, 'Honestly you can.'

'No – it's O.K.'

'Tomorrow then?'

'O.K. Let's go. Boyd, I'll meet you outside – I just want to buy a magazine.'

He is waiting beside an old Chinese woman at the kerb. The crossing light shows red. He touches my sleeve. 'I didn't believe you were' – he hesitates – 'gay. Not even in that place. I thought that was your joke taking me there 'cos I never thought of you as bent 'cos you have a deep voice and that.' The crossing beacon bleeps and the green man lights up. Part-way over he says, 'Christ, Simon! And then you went to buy that gay magazine!' He rolls his head. 'Duckie, duckie, duckie . . . Jeez! *Kinell!* I don't believe it!'

We have both stopped in the centre of the crossing. A car-driver presses his horn and Boyd with sweeping gesture two-fingers the man. 'Up yours!' he shouts. He is wild, black-jacketed, jumping; then he winks at me and runs along the pavement. He shakes his head and calls, 'I don't believe it! Oh, *Kinell!*'

We have been going to the pub together for two weeks now; we have a loyalty as well as a liking for one another. I am responsible for him: when one morning he was ill I had to show him the way to the office sick-bay, then Hannah whispered to me: 'Careful he doesn't drag you into bed.' He didn't – for in the cool green room with curtains moving slightly in the breeze he asked if I didn't honestly prefer women.

Today we go into the town centre to shop for my groceries. This he enjoys and he runs around the supermarket at speed. On the way back he has a short conversation with a girl: I am fascinated by the amount of attention she pays him. She extends an invitation – it is charmingly ignored. She leaves and I ask, 'Why are you so liberal, Boyd?'

'What? What?'

'You don't give a shit if anyone is white or black or gay. You seem to have no prejudices at all. You don't even hate Valerie at work – and she's a bitch.'

'Yeah – I heard her on about how I couldn't walk in my boots. *And* my having no bum at all.'

'You reckon you're good-looking?'

He laughs. 'You won't believe this; one girl told me I was good-looking. I didn't even know her and she came up to me at this disco and told me that. It really surprised me.'

'Hannah reckons you are. She says she can imagine you pink and naked rolling on a rug.'

'Will you marry me?'

'God, you are stupid! If you weren't so stupid you'd be cruel. And stop doing that!'

'What?'

'Gobbing. That's what. You've started doing it recently.'

'It's hygienic.'

'Hygienic? How's it hygienic to expectorate in the lousy street?'

'Do you have a dictionary?'

'Haven't you got a hanky?'

'Dunno. But if I had a hanky and spat into that – that wouldn't be hygienic, would it?' He grins. 'We're very late.'

'Are we?'

'That's you. It's good coming out with you lunchtimes 'cos no one ever dares say anything when we get back late. They daren't – not with you.'

The passageways of the office building are painted light green and there are scuff marks. Once out of sight of the manager's glass-sided room with the three telephones, Boyd mouths: 'Graffiti,' and pretends to scrawl on the wall with his pen. He says, 'What we need is a can of spray paint. A large FUCK in red.' We are both outsiders; we are together and we want to rebel, to scream our frustration, to deface and sometimes destroy. We collide in the entrance door to the carpeted foyer which I call the Quiet Zone; here it is like a time-lock. Before entering our office I whisper outrageously in his ear: 'I think I'm falling in love with you.'

Suddenly Hannah opens the inner door. Boyd is silencing painful laughs. He hangs onto the steel umbrella rack, rolling backwards and forwards. Hannah asks why we are laughing.

I say to Boyd, 'Tell her and you're dead.'

I leave them and go into the lavatory; I run the tap, shut the window – the traffic noise is muffled, and I rest my forehead on the cool tiles. A joke with Boyd – anything for a laugh. The detergent dispenser has a slimy congealed rubbery lump; I push it off and pump hard, lathering my hands. I force myself to look in the mirror. I hate my reflection, hate hair-combing, hate anything involving watching me. I even jump when I catch sight of myself in shop windows. A face unsmiling stares back. There are creases either side of the mouth; the nose has been broken; the mouth is good until it opens, then, close up, the white fillings show in the front teeth and a laugh will reveal extensive dentistry further back. The light from the window thins my hair. I snap at myself, thinking I am not bad to look at, I can console myself with the flattery of Boyd and our humour. But I am the joke – a forty-year-old male with no sexual liking for females. The fillings show when I bare my teeth again.

Valerie stares. She stares out of the window. She stares at the wall. Today she stares at Boyd: it is in these moments of concentration that she dreams of Donald. She is young but seems to despise most young people – she loathes Boyd – but

77

then she loves Donald. As she stares I can overhear her telling Hannah how Donald fixed her washing-machine last night and this evening he is scheduled to paper the lounge ceiling. Donald is a gem. Several times we have been shown the three packs of photographs of Donald on honeymoon in Benidorm. And Hannah and I had great difficulty not cracking up when told that Donald had said she must on no account apply for promotion because he didn't want her working too hard.

She says: 'Hannah? Did you hear that Jill from the typing-pool yesterday? You know what that particular lady is like after lunch with umpteen scotches under her belt and with the fag hanging out of her mouth. She asked the new office manager – and I can scarcely believe it now – if it was true that one lost one's sex drive after one reaches sixty. He's as timid as a church mouse. Donald said I shouldn't mix with that type of person. She's only showing herself up. Donald thought she sounded terribly common.' Valerie continues to stare at Boyd, unaware that both he and I can hear every word she says. 'That Boyd! I told Donald about him and Donald told me not to take any notice of him. In fact, he said he sounded a twat!'

Boyd is delighted. He brings down a ruler sharply on the knuckles of my hand. I flinch and gasp slightly. 'Quite honestly, Simon,' says Boyd loudly, 'if you can't take that you simply aren't a man. And I think personally that you are a bit of a twat.' I find this excruciatingly funny.

Valerie stops talking but still stares fixedly at Boyd.

Boyd says to me, 'I was only thinking, moments ago, what a twat you are.'

I am shaking with laughter, and press my face into my hands. Hannah laughs with her eyes and Boyd leans over and whispers in my ear, 'Twat! Twat!' And I roll on the desk, tears running down my face.

On the familiar street to the King's Head road-sweepers have heaped leaves at regular intervals in the gutters; Boyd runs at them shouting 'Yahoo!' and kicks at each pile. I wait until we round the corner where it is sheltered by small terraced villas before I show him my letter.

'What? What does it mean?' he asks.

'I've got my job back – at sea.'

'You're selfish, Simon. It's good in that office.'

'The work's boring. The ship sails in a couple of weeks. I leave the office on Monday.'

'Have to, don't you?' he shouts. 'Work!' Then he swears angrily and spits into a walled garden. Boyd is the yob now. He runs at speed – like Road Runner with cartoon energy; he turns and runs back reaching me as I stop at the top of the bridge. He leans over the parapet and gobs at a barge passing beneath. The wind catches the phlegm and brings it back, splattering it on the road.

In the pub he behaves himself and as he brings the beers, he says to me, 'See that weirdo at the bar?'

I nod.

'He has one of those small voices, "Hello" and "How are you?" crap. He asked me what my name was. I said, "Can't remember."' He drinks his lager. 'You changed your mind about going back to sea?'

I shake my head. 'It's a great chance. I can escape that office.'

Later that afternoon, after Hannah and Valerie go to tea, Boyd is confidential. 'Simon?'

'What?'

'I've got to tell you something – now.'

'Um.'

'Are you listening?'

'For goodness' sake spit it out!'

'This is serious – it's about Spiff.' He whispers, 'He's here, for Christ's sake! Over there! What a wally with that upper-class haircut!' Boyd continues with drama: 'Spiff asked me just now in the bog why I went out with a queer.' Then thinking, adds, 'That's you.'

It's an impulse reaction that I stand; and once stood I can't sit down again. I have to confront Spiff. I catch him as he leaves the room; I wait until we are in the time-lock – the Quiet Zone. 'Spiff?' He stops, saying nothing. 'I hear that you've been talking about me behind my back.'

'No. No, I haven't.'

'But you have. You called me a queer.'

The face verges on being pretty, the complexion flawless; he might hate his soft skin. 'It's not only me what said it.'

'But you've started to interfere with me. You asked Boyd why he went about with a queer.' He is dying to escape, and moves as if debating whether he can make a break for it; but this he cannot do for I have fixed him quite firmly in the carpeted time-lock. 'I do happen to be homosexual,' I say. A messenger enters, overhears; it as though I have deliberately chosen my timing, for the man hesitates before opening the other door: I wait for him to leave. 'I can't think why it should bother you,' I say.

There is slight colour in his face. 'You said things – spoke of me to Charles.'

'*Charles*? You're kidding! I would never confide in him. He's this building's gutter press; one must never talk to him about anything.' Spiff's eyes aren't bad enough to detract from the face's prettiness. I can't dislike him; he looks too miserable. I continue: 'Charles is a gossip. He told me something about you which I would never repeat to anyone.' I remember Charles's words exactly and they have a ring of truth about them: 'He makes me feel young again.' I can't be bothered with Spiff any more and leave him in the Quiet Zone and return to the office.

After work Boyd and I walk to the bus stop. There is someone running behind us; Charles. He ignores me and says to Boyd, 'Where do you work?' He knows precisely where Boyd works; he has seen him at least a half a dozen times and those gossip, camera-recording eyes could never miss him. Spiff has blabbed. Boyd shrugs his reply – it is a gesture of insolence, but Charles hangs on, 'Whereabouts?'

I am annoyed. 'Shut it, Charles. You know.'

'They're taking in roughs now, are they?' As Charles turns to make the grand exit of the final word, Boyd makes a prolonged farting sound with his mouth and he and I laugh loudly as Charles stalks away.

The young man with the face of the boxer and the stance of a tough moves with grace and speed. He's seldom still. He shows me a snapshot of himself in Marine's uniform; he goes training twice a week and is proud of this. I can visualise him as an N.C.O. shouting orders on a parade ground.

Today he wears a worn-out, grown-out-of anorak of bright

orange and he chatters like a schoolboy. He stops walking and examines me. 'You've got grey hair.'

'Yeah. It's creeping down my body. I'm greying in layers.'

'There's a man at our local who's like a gorilla.'

'I'm not like a goddam gorilla.'

'He has his shirt open all the time. Open your shirt.' I shake my head. 'Christ, you're shy! Show us your leg, then.' I pull up my trouser leg and he rocks silently, laughing at me.

The snooker hall is under trees, and is ice-cold inside. I stand in front of a gas fire and take sips from a bottle of whisky I've brought. Boyd throws me his anorak to hang up; a black leather wallet falls open on the floor, and there are five pounds in it.

'I thought you were broke, Boyd.'

He is startled. 'You lent me the five this morning.'

'Oh, yeah. I remember.'

He shakes his head. 'God, I love you.' He talks while he walks round the table: 'Guess who I met on the train last night.'

'Dunno.'

'*Guess!*'

'I don't know, for Christ's sake!'

'The youngish man who asked your name?'

'Right. Right. Right. That little camp voice. Take the pink – this pocket . . . Christ – you've pocketed it!' He mimics: '"Hello! Where's your friend?"' Then he spots my Marine's uniform under my coat 'cos I've been to drill. He says, "You're a *soldier*! You're in the *army*!" *Kinell*, I nearly died – the carriage being full and that. Then he says for no reason at all in *that* voice: "We gays are human beings, you know."'

'What did you say?' I rest my cue on the table.

'I was struck dumb – the people in the carriage staring out of the window and watching me in the reflection of the glass. And he's got this grand house near the canal and – *Kinell*! Wait for it – he tells me, with all those people hanging on every fucking word, he's looking for *someone* to share it with. I almost died.'

'Boyd, if you don't want whisky – there's beer.'

'Lager. It's lager you've got.'

'Lager is beer. You want one?'

'Only one. I would really like to get p-i-s-s-e-d'– he child-ishly spells out the word – 'but I've got this match with Vince.'

Vince arrives. Boyd is ruthless; he plays to win and pulls further and further ahead. I find I am hoping that Vince will narrow the huge gap. Boyd is superb: he moves about the table outwardly casual – and he stops to chat with me. I am his support, his lucky mascot; it is as though he can't lose while I am here. When the match finishes he follows me outside; the tarmac, no longer black, is covered with snow.

'Thanks for coming and supporting me like that. Thanks a lot.'

It's the first time he's thanked me like that, well, sincerely thanked me, that is.

The man who is about to cut my hair at Bucks is, I am quite certain, the man who used to work at the rival hairdresser's in the High Street. He certainly talks the same way but if I try to put the London accent on the page it would be painful to read. In fact it's great to listen to. Another reason why I think he's the same man is his clothes – they are dreadful. His pants are a thin black material fitted at the waist and extremely full about the hips, tight at the ankles in what I can only hope is a quickly passing fashion. It is his hair which throws me. It's bleached now, but in the early summer it was dark brown.

'Where you work?' he asks.

'I've left my job,' I tell him. 'Back to sea again in a week. Calcutta and Cochin.'

He is smiling and my hair is warm and wet. The palm of his hand rubs at the nape of my neck. I am facing the ceiling with its papered-over cracked plaster; and the back of my neck is in the rest of a porcelain basin. He is using a hand-shower.

'You going out? Tonight, I mean.'

'I hadn't thought.' I would like to think this is a pick-up, but that might be wishful thinking.

'I've left home now,' he says and adds mysteriously, 'I took the chance when it came.'

If I had his lack of inhibition I would have asked what chance; instead I grin at the papered ceiling as he lathers for a second time. 'I'm twenty-two now. Some of my mates are still living at home.' The moustache is dyed white and it matches the hair exactly. He is round front waiting for me to move to the chair where we can talk with each other in the mirror. When he finishes he switches off his blower and is already seducing his next customer. I am being looked after by the woman who takes the money and has earlier made me a bitter coffee. She represents encroaching heterosexuality and makes a great deal of brushing me down; her short chubby, red-nailed fingers pick hairs – I think they are mostly imagined – off my sweater.

'Leave him alone, Jean!' says my hairdresser with the London accent and the dyed moustache. 'He's mine and he said he'd see me in the new club near the station at ten tonight.'

It's Monday lunchtime. I've arranged to meet Boyd in the King's Arms, for tonight I travel to Hull to join my ship.

He is dramatic: 'God, Simon, I'm a marked man now you've left. They've moved me into an office with that Spiff wanker – miles away from Hannah.'

'You'll miss her.'

'I miss you.'

'How'd you mean – exactly?'

He flirts. 'Hell, you know.' He looks evil, dressed in black; he is the bad man in a Western. 'The office manager was on about my time-keeping and my clothes. Why you had to leave, I don't know.' He pauses and waves to the barman. 'Hannah was really, really upset us both leaving. She's stuck with that Valerie who sits there all day like a parrot in a trance, dreaming of darling Donald and staring at the wall.'

A man nods at Boyd.

'You know him?' I ask.

'It's *him*!' hisses Boyd. 'And he can see I'm buying you a drink. Him on the train with the little voice. He's – we gays are all human beings. Remember?'

'Vividly. You've made a catch there.'

'*Kinell*!' He clears his throat noisily, sucking back the phlegm.

'You're disgusting . . . And where did you get that cut?'

'On my face? Don't ask. A fight. What did you do over the

weekend?' The palm of his hand rubs nervously along the smooth edge of the bar counter.

I point at his hand. 'I met someone and we did that.'

'What?' He stares at his hand rhythmically rubbing. 'Christ!'

'You're shocked?'

He grins. 'I didn't expect that. You saying that.'

'You ordered these sandwiches?' The barman recognises Boyd and asks him: 'You're the toasted cheese, my darling?'

When he leaves, Boyd hugs himself and repeats, 'My darling! Listen to him! My darling!'

'The club I visited might interest you. It was part lesbian. I went to the gents and there were two women in there. One squirted me with perfume. When I objected she said, "Well, it is Estée Lauder."'

Boyd's eyes are bright. 'Where is this place? I am so innocent. Where?'

'Near the station in a basement. I remember discarded fish and chip wrappers stuck to my shoes as I went down the steps outside. There was a bell and a peephole and a bouncer.'

'*Kinell!*'

'Bad in the office without me, is it?'

He smiles evilly. 'Horrible! this is our last drink together. Let's get p-i-s-s-e-d.'

His hands are making swirls in the spilled beer on the counter. The wind bangs open the door and its retaining spring pulls it shut again. The man alone at the nearby table is watching Boyd surreptitiously, jealously thinking we are together. Boyd puts his rough hand on my fist and grips hard.

'Drink! Come on – our last drink together!'

DISCOTHÈQUE
– FOUR VOICES

Martin Foreman

Tube noisy, shaky, empty. Old woman beside me, Rasta over there, head-phones on, deaf and blind to the world. In the black window opposite I can almost see me. Hair good, eyes not clear, no, everything is good. I stood in front of mirror and saw strength and arrogance of make-up, clothes and eye. Jacket new, white, training pants white with blue streaks, suggesting energy, sex, life. White is good, shiny white is pure, sexy. Blue is light, blue is life.

Train stops, doors open, yellow light, couple get in. One more stop. I want to be there, to strip off, to dance. I am different. I am me, I can dance, I will dance, I am dance. Others pretend, others play, others sleep, others die, die, die. I live, I do, I dance. My body moves, my body lives, it is long, strong. I live, I dance.

Train stops. Get out. Along platform, up escalator. Others around me, going too. Couples kissing, holding, couples. I am alone. No John. I am now alone. No John. I will always be alone. Punk, denim, no style. I have style. I have style and colour and life and dance. I walk on air. I'm walking on air through dark street. No one can touch me, no one can see me. Everyone can see me, everyone can envy me. I have strength, smoothness, power, attraction, life. I can fly.

Always a queue. Fat, ugly doorman. Bored girl taking money. On and in, on and in. Here, against the wall, by the cloakroom, stop and strip, peel off clothes, watch those watching me, wanting me. They want me, want my body, want my life. Fold jacket, fold pants, put in bag. Hand bag over. I am naked, I am free. I am savage, I am warrior. I come to dance, stomp, circle, burn, celebrate, destroy. I am war-chief, I am king.

On, on. Door opens, light, music, life explodes. I leap up, touch ceiling, stretch out arms and legs and land. I am alive. I twist, I turn. Around me people stand and talk and drink and walk and look and they're dull and drab and dreary. Not everybody. That gold cape, gold hair, gold face. He is trying, but he has buried himself. He does not have style, he does not have life. That girl does, however, that girl who laughs and looks at me. And there is John, with his back to me, same jeans, same stance, same thick curly hair. Then he turns and I see and I know and I remember that John is dead, that John will always be dead.

It is a vast cavern, another world. The gods shine down on us, play for us, call to us. This is eternity, I can stay here for ever. I can dance and dance and learn to fly. Here, where we move and live and laugh and cry, is where I belong. We are the warriors come to celebrate, to dance the dance of life, the dance of death. I am the chief come to sacrifice, the virgin come to die.

They watch, they always watch. They watch my body with its muscles, so clear, so hard, they stare at my briefs, they want my cock, they stare at my legs. John loved my legs. They watch me dance, watch me move, some mock but they all admire. I have the courage to be myself, to be free, to live. So they move apart, let me pass, and I come onto the floor and the lights flash and the music surrounds me and my body begins to move. Legs up, down, left, right, arms out, curve, straight, body hunch, round, straighten arms, legs, armslegsarmsbodyoutleftthumpthumpthump green red green red white green dark green dark green dark red thump thump thump voice, I'll always be there; thump thump snake across snake of light snake of sound thump thump around up back hot thump thump sweat thump thump waterfall of sound thunder of light up up "for you for you for you" thump thump faces arms legs denim black dress stare thump thump thump and on and on and on

I walk slowly, carefully, a model on a catwalk, a cat on a

tight-rope, along corridors, up stairs, round a balcony and back down to the main floor. My eyes are never still, creep like a prowling thief from one person to the next, from face to body to crotch to face. They are my guides and my censors, yet when they approve I do not stop to appraise but walk on, nervous and afraid, seldom turning back to wonder and hope. My courage is truly Dutch – I need alcohol to cruise as a weight-lifter needs his steroids – and the drink I have poured has not yet had time to pore. So I go to the bar and full glass in hand stand at the edge of the dance-floor, looking out to sea and trying to focus on the waves.

A silhouette here, movement there; a bright shirt in the darkness signals and vanishes. I strain into the night and catch only bobbing hair and flickering faces; out of the whirlpool an arm, a body, an expression appear and are dragged down. I focus on a smile and it has soured into a scowl, watch a tee-shirt sag as its strength dissolves, a man vanish where he should stand for ever. Am I growing old or was I never able to see clearly through lights that flash from brilliance to darkness, from point to flood, from one colour to the next, bursts of magic that transform age into youth, beauties into beasts, flesh into fantasy and my despair into desire? It is all as vague as a dream, as vague as the dream lover whom I search and long for. All I can be sure of is those who are near me, those whose reality cannot be denied.

Two men in dresses with painted faces and blinding blond hair clomp energetically. A tall thin individual's moustache is as serious and heavy as the movements he makes. A dark-haired youth in sleeveless shirt pirouettes, bounces, leaps and dives, laughing, grinning, watching his partner. His body is slim, tight, young, he moves with such energy, he is so happy, he would make me laugh, he would bring me tea in bed, would make things and paint things; I want him, I want him, I want him, but he sees only his partner, his lover, his accomplice, a dull man in black who rocks unimaginatively from side to side, watching with the pride and self-satisfaction of possession. If I stood, if I stayed, if I stared, if I stabbed between them with my eyes, letting the ache in my chest, in my mouth, in my groin, pour out, I could not prise them apart, would never see that youth, that wondrous youth, dance for me.

Away. Another round. A policeman on his beat, watching the crowds, the passers-by, the suspicious loiterers, ready to pull one or more in for questioning. I begin to recognise them, to know who I have rejected and who I wish to inspect again. Yet as I walk past I feel and fear their returning stares. Everything is too open, too honest, too searching, too abrupt. I need a two-way mirror so I can watch and choose at my leisure, examine their stance and expression, practise my lines and smile. Then when ready, rehearsed, I could swoop and sweep them away. Instead, all they see and hear is my hesitation, my concentration, my verberation. . .

Open shirt and jeans, ankle boots and ruffled hair. He offers strength and reassurance, quiet drinks in country pubs, pleasant home, a recent car. My courage well and truly screwed, I go and talk and am rewarded by monotonous monosyllables and perfunctory politeness. Yes, no, sometimes, no thank you. A bore, a stuck-up insufferable bore. Sour grapes, sour grapes; you're too old to be angered or hurt by rejection. Move on, move on.

Back at the dance floor the rhythm is faster, the lights brighter. Two hundred, three hundred people together. I look from one to the next like a bee at the end of summer hunting for pollen. One is too old, another's too short, too fat, too feminine, too unfriendly, has the wrong fetish, wrong sex, wrong clothes or expression. The ones I want, the one I want, lurks beyond like a chameleon behind his brethren. A blond in blue shirt and black trousers, a crew-cut, stripped and sweating to the waist, curly hair and warm eyes in incongruous pullover. They shift in and out of my vision, tumbling arms, swinging hips, turning legs, as if I were invisible, as if I did not exist.

My gaze bounces from floor to ceiling, my eyes blur and refocus, searching through the forest of cotton and denim. There a mirage, shimmering in the stormy light, white briefs tight over pumping buttocks, framed by bare back and bare legs. He turns, blue and white make-up streaks from his eyes, dances across his chest, dives into his groin. He is not handsome, but his nose and jaw are strong and sweat drips down his cheeks from his damp and dark hair. He has no expression, is as unseeing as if hypnotised or drugged or mindless. His chest is strong and the sweat flows down, down, over the hollow of his stomach to be absorbed by the band of white. There his cock is veiled, virginal vigilant. He has the legs of a runner and when he turns I can see the ripple of his back-bone, the dancing shoulder-blades and lean hollows of his hips. I want to take him, to have and to hold him, to kiss and lick and stroke and arouse. He would be mine to make as I wish and yet he would never change. He would listen and learn and yet be my teacher. He would lie in my bed, our bed, and be made love to, he would overpower me and make me his. We would fight and forgive, leave and live and love each other. He is everything I desire, he is my desire and he is here before me, he is here for me.

Coming down is not natural, coming down is pain, coming down is returning to life after the oblivion of death. I want to dance for ever, I want to live for ever, I want to forget for ever. John and I danced, John and I danced, when he was tall and strong and loved me and we danced here and made love here and my hips ground into his and I felt his cock; I felt his love and we danced here when he was old and thin and tired and I watched him and could not cry and watched him and could not cry.

Coming down is forced by tiredness and thirst, slipping from the groove. Don't want to leave, but slip, through, out, up to bar. Wait, order drink, wait, turn. They pretend not to watch, but they do, they do. They want my mouth and my nipples and my stomach and my cock, they want to kiss my legs, to run their hands up, to run their hands up, to feel the muscles, to feel the hair, to grasp, to stroke; they want to reach slowly up, to hear my gasp, to feel the ache, the desire, they want their mouths on my cock, I want John's mouth on my cock, they want to suck, to suck my life from me.

I won't, I can't, I won't, I can't. I am John's, I can only be John's. I will not be theirs, I cannot be theirs. If only there were another John, but there isn't another John, there will never be another John.

Someone talks, I turn. Tall, dark, balding, putting on weight, trying to impress, wanting to reach out, put his hand on my body, John's body. He talks and talks. The same words, always the same words. He has nothing, he is nothing. Finish drink, smile. Back to dance-floor. Wait, look round, perhaps someone. . . No, never, dance, dance, dance.

If the figures aren't on my desk by lunchtime, she will have to go. I don't care what personal problems she has, they can't interfere with business. I shouldn't have taken her on in the first place, but these agencies are so bloody persistent. All they're interested in is their commission. 'Mr Wright, we've found someone who's ideal for you. She's been two years with Securicor and is looking for a more responsible position.' Or whatever they said. They all sound as wonderful as their own adverts. And I was taken in. She was very smart, very competent at the interview. There was no reason not to hire her. And then I discover she's paranoid, neurotic, incapable, loses files, forgets appointments, thinks the other girls are down on her, calls in sick every other week, and I have to put in time doing my own secretary's job.

Another drink. It's always the third one that brings me down to earth, that makes the office seem less important, that convinces me for a time that it does not matter that we have been making a loss for over a year, that it is my job to cut expenditure, to tell Derek and Roger we cannot afford this or that. It's not Roger that's the problem, it's Derek. He hates my guts, he's looking for an excuse to get rid of me. I have to be careful, because if I lose this job, God knows where I'll find another. No one wants a middle-aged rat from a sinking ship.

Well, perhaps today it's the fourth drink that'll remind me it's half past midnight and I'm in a discothèque and what I need is a really good fuck. There are some quite attractive faces and bodies around if I can remember to look at them, maybe even smile and talk and I'll forget about the office and Andrew at home.

Andrew at home. Or Andrew at a disco, this disco, maybe I'll see him here. No, I won't. It would be beneath him. This is the kind of place he'd go to a few times at university, as he'd smoke pot and sleep with one or two women to see what it's like and be patronising about it for the rest for his life. God, he's become intolerant. No, that's not true. He's always been intolerant; I just used to admire it, think it was strength of character. A strong personality, a sense of humour and loving nature, that's what I bought a house with. And what have I got now? An intolerant cynic who suspects me of screwing with every man who looks at me twice. Who'll either be awake when I get in or who'll make bitchy comments first thing in the morning. And he thinks it's adolescent to go to discos!

I just need to get laid. Have another drink. Forget work, forget Andrew, forget everything and find a man. Five drinks since I came in. I have to stop.

How long has he been beside me? I expect people to be outrageously dressed in here, but not like that. Look at the sweat dripping down him, look at those muscles, look at that basket. He's practically naked; all I need do is hook my finger in there and pull down and. . . He must be available. He wouldn't be dressed like that, undressed like that, otherwise. He wants to be picked up, he wants to be taken home and fucked. And I want to be the one to do it, even if it costs me fifty, a hundred. He won't refuse. He needs it; whether it's the sex or the money, he needs it.

You must be hot. Been dancing a lot. I like the colours; does the design mean anything? I thought maybe it was something to do with Red Indians. It's not very busy tonight. I haven't seen you here before. It's been a long day for me, how about you? Like a drink? Where do you live? Are you doing anything later? Maybe I can give you a ride home.

He may walk away, he may think he's turned me down, that I'll take the hint, that I'll go and find some pretty little teenager who'll be glad of an extra thirty or forty quid. But I don't want a doll. I want a man. I want him and I'm going to get him. He's gone to the dance-floor. I'll follow and stand and watch and stare at him, until he gets used to the idea. Because that's what he wants, that's why he's dressed like that, even if he doesn't know it. It's an open invitation to anyone and I'm going to make sure I'm the one to get it.

There he is in the centre. Easily visible, despite the irritating flashing lights and all the others around him. No one else seems to notice him. Not true; I can see one or two with their eyes on him. He dances well, with the music, with variety.

That body can move, the hips grind, pump, thrust. I want to take him like that, sweaty, tired, out of breath, not quite sure where he is, throw him over my desk, rip off his pants and fuck him in the middle of the reports and the unanswered letters and the forward accounts, fuck him so that he shouts and brings that stupid woman in to shriek and throw up her hands in horror, fuck him so that the whole room shakes, the oh-so-decorative plants by the window fall off their stand and crash through the glass, fuck him as if he were Derek or Andrew screaming for mercy, fuck him so hard that the whole building collapses around us, fuck him so hard that nothing in the world is left except him and me.

My head expands, my body glows. I am the king, I am the warrior, I am the virgin. I am free, I am music, I am light, I am strong, I am sex, I am life, I am me. I move, I am naked, I am God, God moves, I move, my armslegsbody move, I am cock, I am arse, I am cock, hard, thrusting, I am arse, open, welcoming, I am all they desire, I am movement, I am energy, I am light. I dance, I fuck, I dance, I am fucked. With John I fucked, he loved my body, I loved his body, before, before, before. He was strong, he was handsome, not thin, not thin and old. I don't want to remember, I don't want to remember. Move, move, move, up, down, round, free, I am free, I am free.

I am two minds, one dances, the other watches. One is free, one is laughing. They see and pretend not to see. They want and pretend not to want. They want to fuck, I want to fuck, but not with them, not with them. My cock and arse are my heart, my soul, my all. They want but they cannot have. The white cloth, the chastity, the purity protects, protects and reveals. What they want and cannot have. I am vulnerable and I am free.

They approach, hungry eyes, desperate eyes, dance around me, dance at me, want me want me want me but I am not here, I do not want, I am, I dance, I dance. He dances too, tries to hold me with his eyes, happy eyes, and shirt and jeans. He is a mirror, his eyes follow him, his legs follow mine, his arms follow mine. He wants me. Yes, maybe, perhaps, one day. One day in the future, a long time from now, you and I, you and I.

But not today, not tonight; I am not here. I am music, the light, the dance. I am not here. I am free, I am strength, I am sweat, I am sex, I am free.

On and on and on and on. My life myself I exist this is me, this is me, this is me. Nothing before, nothing after. No John. No illness and death, no tears and pain, no love, no love, no love. I want, he is gone gone gone. I am alone I am now I am nothing nothing before nothing after. Black black black silent silent silent still still on on on

Sometimes those two go over the top. A joke's a joke but if it were a cow they'd milk its corpse. It's time I left them alone and went for a walk to see what's on offer tonight. I didn't come here to listen to their double act. I suppose I came to look around, see if there's anything interesting and if there was pick him up. Maybe just to talk, not even have sex! How times have changed; I remember sitting on old Uncle Michael's knee, listening wide-eyed and open-mouthed to his tales of Islington cottage. 'There was one old queen who used to turn up every evening, take his false teeth out, slip them into his pocket and stuff a cushion under his knees. There'd be a queue out onto the pavement and always one local bobby on his way back to the nick. With his helmet off, of course, so one one would recognise him.'

Stop it. You're getting as bad as the others. Well, what have we here? I thought the cowboy look died with Ronald Reagan's last coherent sentence. Or maybe he's up from some weird club in the East End. Doesn't he know it's the tramp look these days? Unshaven, long dirty coats, and a look of dementia or debility. And that's just the women.

Stop it! Be serious. Look through this assembly of masculinity in all its variety and choose the one that's suitable for *you*. I mean, somewhere out there there must be someone six feet tall, twenty-three or thereabouts, with the mind of Einstein, the wit of Coward and the looks of Tom Cruise, whose one aim in life is to meet and fall passionately in love with the manager of a pet shop and the proud possessor of a Mini that's had more spent on it in repairs in the last month than it was ever worth when it was new. Not to mention the menagerie at home and the flatmate who insists on playing classical music at the volume of Heavy Metal.

Now that one's very attractive. Well, the body could do with a bit of an overhaul, but I like the face. Sort of cute and knowing. The kind of guy who'd send embarrass-the-boss telegrams and swear he had nothing to do with it. But he's with someone. Onto the next. And very quickly onto the one after that; why do some people assume that a leather jockstrap makes even the scraggiest body desirable? There should be a law against it. There probably is.

I watched that one earlier in the evening. It's not so much the face but the way he dresses – trendy enough to show he knows what he's doing, but not so trendy that he doesn't have a mind of his own. He even smiled. I should have gone over then. But now he's talking to someone; maybe he was with him all the time. It's too late, too late, all the best fruit has gone.

Well, who needs sex anyway? Quarter of an hour on the dance-floor is just as satisfying. More so, because you can do whatever you want. Not that I'm a great dancer. In fact I prefer dancing alone. There's nothing more embarrassing or stupid than to dance with someone for half an hour and not once look him in the eye. You might as well dance alone. So, squeeze into the middle, try not to get hit by that drunken woman or that skinhead who looks as if he's had constipation for a week, find yourself a space and shake yourself about a bit.

Why is it the more attractive ones are always taken up? O.K., I know it's not true; I just need an excuse. I mean that boy in the white tee-shirt. He probably works out three times a week, looks as if he's intelligent, moves as if he's good in bed and is staring into his lover's eyes as if hypnotised. Turn round, look elsewhere. Oh, cheeky! Does he want us to think he's walked off the beach? And what's that he's got on his body and face? O.K., admit it, the colour's striking. So's he. And, it seems, alone. I'll bet you no one's had the courage to go up and talk to him. Beauty often puts people off. And he is, well, not beautiful. Hunky, gorgeous, sexy, built, and, from the looks of it, hung. Who cares if his face won't launch a thousand ships? Look at those thighs, that chest, that etcetera.

Faint heart never won hunky youth. Get over there, dance with him. That's what he likes, that's what he understands. Go and strut your stuff, do your thing, stare him out, draw him on. No one else is. Let yourself go. Just dance. Don't stare at him, don't think about him, relax, let the music take over, be aware, that's all, be aware, feel your body sway, your arms surge, your legs pound and pound and turn and leap and launch and see him, see his muscles, see them flex and stretch and curve, and he is dancing and I am dancing fast and my eyes are half-closed and his hips move from side to side and I move with him and his backside seems to grind into my groin and he turns and leans back and offers me his cock and I could reach out and take it but that would be going too far and I swing with him and there is only darkness with torchlight flashing from the ceiling and the music is fast, fast and I look at him and he seems to be smiling and his back is to me again, moving faster than I ever could and he turns and I look at him and we dance together and as I move in one direction he moves in the other, too fast for me, too flexible, too energetic and we move together and he moves apart and I turn and he is further away and I look at him and he doesn't see me and another body comes between us and the music has caught me and I can't stop, I dance and I dance and I dance and so does he but he is further away and there is someone between us and he does not care, he never cared.

I dance alone. Maybe I expect too much. I should wait until he is tired, comes off for a rest, or wait until the end, talk to him then. I'll just stand at the edge of the floor, watching. He'll get tired, he'll come off sometime. And then we can talk or have a drink or do whatever he wants to do.

On and on and on. Light and music, light and music, red, green, white, blue, red, green blue white red black redblackred thump, thump, thump, layers of music like layers of earth, layers of river flowing at different speeds, deep sounds, dark sounds, shallow sounds, light sounds, on into the sea, into oblivion, into death, round and round, reach and point, thump and thump, sense muscles, sense movement, sense sweat, thump, thump, from hair to toes, swirl, dive and surge, dive and surge. Others around, frozen water, frozen movement, camera caught, back and shoulders, faces and hair, awkward, graceful, watching, ignoring, thump thump thump

Thirsty, want to drink, want to piss, can't stop, must dance, must move, must leap must dance must dance. What's the time where am I who am I what am I I I. I am river I am warrior I am light I am music I am movement. Body sex movement sex movement movement movement. Someone watching, always watching, good, good. Dance more, dance faster. Still there, always there, dancing with me, dancing around me. Jeans, red shirt, red belt red belt. Go away, stay, go away, go stay go stay go stay. Dancing with me I dance faster, fucking with me I fuck faster. He wants my body, my tits, my cock, my arse, he wants me. Fuck off fuck off fuck fuck fuck. So close I can touch him dance him fuck him. His face his face round, wanting, funny, bright, eyes, bright eyes. But he isn't John, I can't reach him, I mustn't reach him, I don't want him, jeans, belt, shirt, red, dark blue, red, dark blue.

I dance with John, only John, I fuck with John, only John. Strong John, kind John, thin John, dying John, dance, dance. John loved me, John loves me, John loves me, John here, John dying, John moving spinning shouting leaping laughing holding kissing stroking kissing fucking kissing falling kissing crying kissing ill kissing ill ill ill

He never stops. He dances on and on like a vision come to haunt me. His hair is matted, his body soaked, the make-up patchy and no one sees him except me and I stand on the sidelines like a spectator at a football match, like a boy on the shore, as if there were a great gulf between us that I could never cross. And if I spend all evening doing this he will never notice me, will walk off when the music stops, stride past me as if I were no more than a scattered chair, a fallen glass. If I want him I have to go after him. I have to get in there, get in and place myself in front of him, so that he sees me, he knows me and then and then. . .

Two hundred pounds. Whatever he wants he can have, but I must have him. I want that body. The world can go hang, Andrew can throw a fit, the firm can collapse tomorrow, but I want that body. I want to have it, to fuck it, to rape it, to have him begging for more, to have him down on his knees, crying, pleading, desperate. And I will pay; whatever it takes I will pay. But I have to have him. I will go over there and stop him. No one ever got what they wanted by waiting for the other chap to snap it up.

Still jiving. And I have to stand here catching my breath. You're out of condition, old son. Remember the days when you could knock back ten pints, knock off ten houses, knock up ten birds, knock down ten cars and still run a four-minute mile? What you need is a Bullworker. Or a bull. Or at least a stud. Or that stud. He is definitely cute, would grace anybody's black satin sheets. So get back in there, dance with him again. He's really desperate for you, he's drooling over your overweight body. He's just shy; these strong silent types usually are. Einsteins in Schwarzenegger bodies never have any self-confidence. Go back, smile sweetly at him, pick him up in your arms and walk, stagger, gracefully off the floor.

Faster faster faster I am music I am light I am light I am everything I am everywhere I am I am I am John my muscles live my body lives I live I die I am I dance I am I I I I . . .

My stomach feels like stone.

I could set him up. Give him a flat. The money'll come from somewhere.

Come on boy, come to Daddy, come on home.

Wet hot blind flash thump thump thump thump . . .

He's a god.

He's it.

He's ill.

John eyes John dies the music dies eyes giant's voice light light whirlwind dies room spins thump thump a face faces I live I die he smiles I smile he they I

He

    collapses

        to the floor.

DISCIPLES

Charles Lambert

His Christian name was Roger. I didn't discover until later, almost seven years after the garage-door affair, just how amusing that was. I remember standing beneath a hump-backed bridge with a boy from school, whose talent it was to find out these things from his elder brother. I listened with delight as he told me what rogering meant. It didn't matter that he had it wrong; what amused me most was how inappropriate it seemed. I couldn't imagine Roger rogering, nor, for that matter, being rogered. The simple idea of him naked was beyond me. His body seemed to end abruptly at the fleshy neck, the line where his flannel shorts cut into his thighs, his dimpled, grasping hands. Roger had nothing to do with sex at all. He was the kind of boy who would hide his snot in the turn-ups of others, and then deny it. He was good at denying; it was second nature to him. That's what rogering should have meant, I thought, flatly denying it. That was how he tried to wriggle out of the garage-door affair.

It happened one afternoon when I must have been four or five, and Roger was about ten. His parents were visiting mine and Roger had been told to give me a box of wooden building blocks that he had outgrown. I remember his reluctance. We argued because he insisted on showing me how to use them, pushing my little hands away, knocking my castle to the floor. I think he hit me, or I hit him. Our mothers defended their children with vigour, our disagreement gradually absorbed by theirs, and we were finally sent outside to play. That's how I remember it, at least. Yet it might not be a memory at all; it might be fragments picked up from listening to my mother while she talked to others. It was the kind of story she loved, a touch of grand guignol, a moral. Or maybe I remember everything just as it was, but have tried to shift it into the clarity of narrative. Either way Roger emerges as the villain of the piece. It went like this.

My mother and father were sitting in the living room with Roger's parents when they heard a piercing scream from outside the window, followed by a series of loud, hysterical sobs. Roger had wandered back into the room some moments before and was eating a slice of Victoria sponge with an air of stubborn innocence. After glancing frantically round the room my father leaped to his feet and demanded to know where I was, but (and this must be my mother speaking) Roger shrugged and took another bite. My father ran out of the house into the courtyard and found me sitting on the gravel drive in front of the garage with the fingers of my right hand trapped in its concertina-styled door. I was drained of colour, too much in pain to cry. He dragged the door open and the sudden rush of blood into my fingers was a new agony. I screamed as he scooped me up in his arms and, sobbing himself, he ran back into the living room. My fingers were flat, like something out of a cartoon. It took days for them to get their shape back.

My mother and Roger's parents were milling round Roger, who was still crouched on the floor, eating determinedly. Grabbing me out of my father's arms, my mother began to rock me clumsily, crying and kissing my bloodless, two-dimensional fingers as the colour came back to them. My father swooped across the room, grabbed Roger by the arms and began to shake him. I remember a swirl of crumbs falling down onto the carpet. At this point Roger's mother seized my father's coat and pulled him, with Roger wriggling and twisting in his grip. Roger's feet were lifted off the floor; his fat red legs kicked out at my father and then went limp, dangling like a doll's limbs. Roger's father had sat down again. He was watching the scene with glazed eyes, a kind of human vacuum. It was ages before anybody spoke.

What made it all so terrible, my mother always said, was not that Roger denied having trapped my fingers in the garage door. I can still remember her shouting 'Liar! Liar!'

until Roger's mother ordered her to shut up. It was the look of unveiled hatred he gave me, as though he had been betrayed and I would have to pay for it. It appeared that I had promised not to tell. And yet my silence itself was a kind of treachery.

The scene must have looked like one of those Victorian genre paintings. The Boy Accused. The weeping mothers in the foreground, one with her arm round her hard-faced child's shoulders and the other with the weeping little victim in her arms. Framing them from behind, the suddenly ineffectual fathers.

I didn't see Roger again for some years. But our families kept in touch and now and again my mother told me stories about him, stories that began to have the air of legend. He was notorious at primary school for scratching. Furious parents would drag their children round to Roger's house to display raised weals on their arms and faces. Roger would rarely confess and, when he did, he seemed to be conferring a gift. He was also, apparently, an accomplished pincher, leaving a stinging pain but no marks. But my mother's favourite story about him involved two Pakistani boys who had come to live next door. After playing with Roger one afternoon they had both gone home with violent headaches, followed by hallucinations. A doctor confirmed that they had been taking drugs and discovered that Roger had made them eat certain tablets "to join his club." They were the first Pakistani family to move into the area and enough remained of their wary awe for Roger's mother to hush the story up. I don't know if he was ever punished, but I doubt it. His mother loved him so much she almost seemed to regard him as miraculous. She once confessed to my mother that she had no real notion how the child had been conceived, since she had "never really let Derek do that kind of thing." Roger seemed to share her sense of wonder.

Despite, or perhaps because of, his penchant for torture Roger became a prefect at the local grammar school and later won an Exhibition to Cambridge to read modern languages. I saw him only once during his student years, towards the end of his first summer vacation. My mother and I went by bus to his house on the other side of town. I remember being taken upstairs and sitting in his drably tidy bedroom while he played me selections of sixties hits, recorded from the radio each Saturday evening with the determined passion of an entomologist. He catalogued the charts in a series of numbered and neatly stacked school exercise-books. Perhaps "passion" isn't the word. It was a kind of camouflage for him. It helped him blend.

His other hobby was Dickens. He was a member of the Dickens Society and, like most of its members, appeared to believe that Martin Chuzzlewit had once both lived and breathed. He was widely read in a bloodless, self-seeking way, although it never occurred to him to question book lists or read beyond them. He was the first person I had ever heard pronounce Goethe, a word I had previously rhymed in my head with the last two syllables of Hiawatha. Perched on the edge of his stiffly-made bed, listening to snatches of Dusty Springfield, I understood that he was trying to seduce me.

The idea of seduction charmed me, but Roger didn't. Growing up had transformed him into a larger and redder version of himself as a boy. I looked at him and thought of the older boys at school. I had dreamed of afternoons like this with sixth-formers, a gradual shift onto the bed as the conversation became more intimate, a hand upon the leg, a kiss. I thought of rugby shorts and the smell of showers, the firmness of arms and legs and necks. But Roger's flesh reminded me of those rubber rings that are used to seal jars of home-made chutney. He talked about Cambridge with an awe-struck air, as though he had never been there himself. I wondered if he had ever seduced anyone there. It seemed unlikely. This was the period during which I discovered Christopher Isherwood and the idea of university as a sexual theme-park, however veiled. It didn't occur to me until later that university might serve any other purpose.

When Roger found out that I was about to apply to Cambridge myself he saw his opportunity.

We drove down with his parents during the summer vacation after his teaching certificate year. I sat in the back of the car with his father, who rarely spoke. Roger and his mother ripped into their neighbours' social pretensions and any dissent from behind was rapidly crushed. Roger's favourite word at the time was "upstart" as though his conservatism applied to everyone but himself. Approaching Cambridge he delivered a damning monologue on the politics of envy. It was during this journey that I learned of his plan to become a public school master.

As soon as we had arrived Roger left his parents in a tea-room and took me to meet his tutor, an elegant man who clearly regarded his former pupil with some contempt. He had written on Jane Austen and had a steely old-maidliness that unnerved me. Roger's accent shifted up, in acknowledgement of his tutor's vowels. I was silent in the airy, light-filled room with its empty fireplace, flattered and disturbed by the attention I was being paid. Tea was brought in by a college servant, who looked at no one. Roger's final, timid hand on my leg was for his tutor's benefit, a rite of passage. I was being transferred, it seemed, a disciple from master to master. The older man said he hoped to see me in October. I smiled. I had already decided to apply to another college.

That trip was the last time I saw Roger alone. He was hurt by my ingratitude when he heard I had chosen another college. His hurt had turned to irritation when I won a scholarship, hiding his bushel beneath my light. Coincidentally, one of my first friends had been in the third form of Roger's grammar school. He told me appalling tales of penknives, spite, interrogation. As a prefect Roger had made him kiss another boy's naked bottom, shaming them both into silence. He had a little group of toadies, whose homework he corrected in return for information. The more Danny told me about him the more I began to see it as my duty to expose him, to himself at least. When he wrote to say that he intended to visit me with another one of his protégés I decided to put on a show.

I had a reputation in college for being out, a reputation I had won by badge-wearing, mild cross-dressing and a flamboyant taste for inhibition-suppressing drugs. I was seen as "politicised," even though I had still not spoken about sex to my parents nor, indeed, considered doing so. I thought I was safe because my exposure was limited to what I understood to be "my life." Nobody, in other words, had been hurt. On the morning of Roger's visit I was wearing black nail varnish, a pair of tartan trousers and beads. Both my ears had been pierced by this time. Tiny gold crosses dangled from sleepers. The room was filled with people, including Danny. *Grundrisse* lay on the table, along with a catalogue of German self-mutilation artists and a copy of Andy Warhol's *Interview*. Ziggy Stardust peered out from his telephone kiosk above my desk.

Lou Reed was singing *Vicious* when the knock came on the door. We had all been smoking and my head was curiously empty as I walked across the room and let Roger in. He stood there in the half-light – I had drawn the curtains. He was wearing a grey suit, white nylon shirt, his college tie. Behind him, moving from one foot to another in a nervous way, was a younger boy in jeans and a sports jacket. Roger was pale. He looked round the room for somewhere to sit, but no one moved, and he finally perched on the arm of a low wooden sofa. His protégé stood behind him, staring with curiosity at the joint that was being passed round. Roger opened his mouth to speak, but couldn't. He was white with rage, as though the colour had been squeezed out of him. I offered coffee, but my offer was refused.

I realised that Roger's plan had been to deliver his new disciple into my hands. I would have held them out to receive him if Roger hadn't so obviously changed his mind. After a moment he began to talk about my parents. I shrugged. I said that I hadn't heard from them for some time. Danny giggled and Roger glanced at him, but failed to recognise his third-form victim. Somebody changed the record. I offered Roger the joint. I chattered facetiously until he stood up to go, walking stiffly towards the door, barely able to say goodbye. As they left the room I gave them both copies of a poetry magazine we had edited, in reparation.

It was not until I was about to close the door behind him that he turned to face me. I looked into his eyes and saw the expression I had seen there, fifteen years before, in my parents' living room, and I realised that I had betrayed him once again. I closed the door.

Ten minutes later another friend arrived. He said that

someone was ripping up copies of our magazine in the court below. Everyone laughed hysterically.

Two weeks after Roger's visit, when I had forgotten all about it, I received a message to call my mother. She was vague and distant at first, and I wondered why she wanted to speak to me. Finally, with difficulty, she said that Roger had been in touch with her. She said that he had felt it was his duty to inform her of the life I was leading at university. She said that he had told her things she couldn't bear. After a while she began to cry. When I tried to explain my life to her she called me a liar, repeating the word in a breathless tearful way until I dried up. What I had done to Roger with silence he had done to me with words.

THE PLAY'S THE THING

Edwin Preece

I don't know why they do it, these regional theatre companies; four weeks before Christmas and they decide to put on a touring production of *Hamlet*. The end of November and we could all do with a nice Rogers and Hammerstein musical to cheer us up, or even an Alan Ayckbourn, but, no, they have to present Shakespeare. Full of people we've never heard of and are never likely to see again, except perhaps in the odd lager advert.

Any whiff of Shakespeare immediately attracts my friend Melvyn. Melvyn works for the local university, drives a CV, wears glasses when reading, watching or listening to anything he considers cultured. He never thinks of turning the heat up in his flat but will instead throw away vast sums of money in either the local bookshop or the small seventies-built theatre that is situated nearby. He rang me late Sunday evening to tell me that Monday was two for the price of one night, and did I mind going with him? As there was a good Agatha Christie about to start on TV, and I didn't want to miss the beginning, I hurriedly said 'Yes,' and put the phone down.

I met Melvyn outside the theatre. He was very excited as he had managed to get tickets in the third row of the stalls. I was less excited as (a) the performance started at seven o'clock and I had to come straight from work, eating a less than fresh salad roll as I made the best of rush-hour public transport, and (b) I learned from Melvyn that the performance didn't end until a quarter past eleven. A long test of endurance, as presumably there would be no production numbers in the Oklahoma mould.

We made our way into the auditorium which was fractionally colder than Melvyn's flat, and although we were sitting in the third row he made a big show of putting on his glasses and looking at the stage, which of course was bare. I looked at my watch. It was five to seven. I opened the programme that we had bought on our way in and it informed me that the theatre seated six hundred people. Unless another five hundred and eighty people all keen to make the most of the two-for-one bargain ticket offer were besieging the box office as I spoke, we were unlikely to be cramped. Scanning the programme I found that the cast outnumbered us by five. The front two rows were empty except for a dirty old man in a raincoat who, Melvyn assured me, was the theatre critic of the local newspaper. I looked behind me to see various small groups of people dotted around the stalls like distant settlements in the Australian outback. Why didn't the box office just seat us all together in the first two rows? If we didn't look behind us, we could then have pretended the place was full, or if things got really boring we could join hands and hold a seance.

I refrained from asking Melvyn too many questions that started with 'How long will it be until?' lest he think I was half-hearted in my approach to the evening. My heart sank as I watched him reach deep into his long black overcoat, the one with the dog hairs all over it, and produce a hardback copy of the play which he proceeded to follow throughout the performance. The house lights went down and various exceedingly loud trumpet sounds came through the speakers as the engineer quickly tried to find the correct levels. Several lights came up on the bare stage, although not all at once. Bernardo and Francisco entered, carrying spears and looking rather self-conscious, and Scene One was under way. Only another nineteen to go, I glumly said to myself.

Scene One lumbered on, enlivened only by the late arrival of four people who tried to fit into three seats due to the under-counting of the first person to enter the row. When they had finally sorted things out, one of them started to undo a large box of chocolates, got the cellophane wrapping caught in the lid and consigned most of the contents to various

107

parts of the stalls. By the time their giggling fit and mine had subsided, another rather ungainly lighting change and a slightly slow-running tape of more trumpets heralded the start of Scene Two.

The impact of Scene Two on me was electric. I sat bolt upright in my seat, riveted to the action on the stage. I couldn't take my eyes off what was happening. Sadly this hadn't anything to do with the standard of the production, although it had everything to do with Hamlet.

While Claudius was droning on, expressing his thanks to his courtiers, I was heavily into a visual appraisal of his nephew. Although he wasn't standing in a pool of light (in fact all the cast seemed to be in shadow – Melvyn was later to call it one of the hallmarks of the production), Hamlet looked stunning. Obviously the fashion of twelfth-century Denmark was designed to suit those of muscular thigh and deep-set chest. Ignoring the King's speech, I discreetly thumbed through the programme until I got to the cast list. I found Hamlet and followed the dots across the page:

HAMLET .... Sean Whitmore

Sean stood at a slight angle on the right-hand side of the stage and I couldn't look anywhere else. Dressed only in a black jacket that came to rest on the top of his thighs, and a pair of tights with some rather nondescript black shoes, he looked stunning. The jacket with its very broad and plunging V shape promised a lot more bare flesh than was actually visible. Despite the advantage of being dressed as a twelfth-century Dane, he had a very modern hair-cut which focused my attention on his thick blond hair. The tights also revealed the extent of his thigh muscles which moved in a fascinating series of bulges whenever he was required to strut around the stage.

I visibly jumped as he spoke to Claudius: 'Not so, my lord, I am too much in the sun.'

Well, I could see that. His face and the part of his chest that I could see still had remnants of a summer tan. Whoever was responsible for costumes obviously thought it was fun to design a top that almost showed the outline of his chest but didn't quite move sufficiently to reveal it all. Still, it did keep me fascinated for the next four acts. By the time Sean arrived in Act Two to proclaim 'What a piece of work is a man!' it was all that I could do to stop myself standing up and shouting 'Ra-ra-ra!'

At half time (or the interval as Melvyn prefers to call it) I was besotted, and when eleven o'clock arrived and Sean died after taking the poison I'm afraid my sobs vibrated around the entire stalls. The rest definitely wasn't silence as far as I was concerned. At the end of the performance the applause from the third row was louder than anywhere else in the whole theatre. Melvyn thought the whole production a fine example of creative minimalism. As the set consisted of three milk crates and a tea-chest wrapped in orange crêpe paper I had to agree with him. We walked home and he gave me what he considered to be a fascinating account of the themes of the play: revenge, honour and the state of the nation. The conversation reached a high point when, crossing the road by some traffic lights, I plucked up enough courage to come clean about the thought that had been obsessing me most of the evening. 'Do you think Hamlet was gay?' I asked.

Melvyn slowed down and carefully stroked his chin. 'It's an interesting concept but I don't think it's ever been played that way before,' he answered vaguely. I, however, spent the rest of the night thinking about Sean, the blond hair, the bulging thighs, the promise of a deep-set chest, which is why the next morning at work I phoned the box office and booked a seat for that evening.

I became obsessed with Hamlet. I even bought a copy of the play! I watched Sean as intently the second night as I had the first, and by the end of Tuesday evening I'd decided to feign illness at work the next day, leave at lunchtime, and book a seat for the afternoon matinée. This was less than successful as I had to share Sean with about five hundred schoolchildren, many of whom were obviously as wild about his body as I was, judging by the wolf-whistles and sighs that greeted his every entrance. I took some solace in the fact that when the poison overcame him I was not the only one sobbing uncontrollably.

After the matinée I threw caution to the winds and booked myself a seat for all the remaining performances of the week. By the end of Thursday evening I knew I just had to meet him;

I had to speak to him, maybe ask him out for a drink. I walked home and decided that after the Friday evening performance I would wait outside the stage door, and when he came out I would casually engage him in conversation and ask him if he'd like to unwind in a pub. It was a pleasant walk home, toying with the idea and rehearsing how I would casually throw into our conversation the offer of a drink. It was only when I arrived back at the flat that I felt a cold chill of reality creeping into the fantasy. It was one thing to play around with the idea in my mind; it was quite another to stand outside the stage door and actually do it.

I had just got home when the telephone started to ring. I picked up the receiver: Melvyn. 'Hello,' he said, somewhat sharply. 'I've been trying to get hold of you since Monday. Where have you been?'

'Evening classes,' I replied flippantly.

There was a slight pause. Melvyn, sensing that I wasn't going to volunteer any further information, carried on. 'The reason I'm ringing is to see if you want to go to Club 49 on Saturday night. They're having a Judy Garland competition. You have to dress up as Judy, of course, and sing one of her songs.'

'Are you entering?' I asked, knowing in all seriousness that Melvyn might enter if it was a Sing-along-with-Kafka night, but he would be hard pushed to name two of Judy Garland's songs, let alone hum them.

'Don't be silly, David.' He always called me David when he was cross. 'A friend from the university's Drama Department is entering and I thought it might be fun to go along and watch.'

It was kind of him to think of inviting me, and I did like the atmosphere at Club 49 although I hadn't been there for some months. I mellowed and even let him talk me into walking around the shops with him on Saturday morning. This still gave me plenty of time to catch the final two performances of *Hamlet*.

Friday night's performance made me aware of how much of the play I was becoming familiar with; I could remember great chunks of it. However, during Act Four I suffered a severe attack of anxiety about what might happen outside the stage door later that night. He might walk out with a group of friends and I'd be unable to say anything; he might walk out and meet his wife, his boyfriend, his mother, his landlord, his pet poodle ... my mind was beginning to wander. Silently I began rehearsing my nonchalant invitation for a post-performance drink. It was increasingly apparent that what I had planned as an off-hand and spontaneous remark would now sound stilted, over-written and over-rehearsed. All through the final act I tried to calm my nerves. As the house lights went up at the end of the performance, I made my way quickly out of a side exit and round the back of the theatre to the stage door.

Oh, Sean, 'For me, or not for me, that is the question!'

I waited by the stage door for well over three quarters of an hour and to my absolute amazement, nobody came out. I even went round to the front of the theatre to see if the cast were leaving through the foyer. I didn't see a soul, and so, somewhat forlornly, I made my way home.

The next morning was a disaster: I overslept and was late meeting Melvyn outside the Town Hall. He was annoyed, as he had already arranged our morning shopping expedition, and hurried me along the street to the alternative book and coffee shop near the market. As usual we made straight for the Drama section. I knew he'd be there ages. I looked round; there wasn't even a chair to sit on. Melvyn was searching for some obscure Greek play that he claimed was a comedy, although when he explained the plot to me it didn't sound like my idea of fun.

I picked up a copy of *The Boys In The Band* I'd come across a few weeks ago when we were last in here and I started to leaf through it. Melvyn sidled up close to me, clutching his rare Greek comedy. 'Have you seen who's in the Gay section?' He nodded his head towards the shelves containing all the books, magazines, information and leaflets that the owners of the shop deemed to be gay. 'It's Sean Whitmore.'

I dropped *The Boys In the Band* and moved trance-like over to where he was standing. Melvyn, carefully stepping over the book, followed. It *was* Sean. I recognised the shock of blond hair as soon as Melvyn pointed him out, although he seemed somewhat shorter than he appeared to be on stage. This was the perfect opportunity and I wasn't going to miss it! As I approached him he looked up and caught me very directly in the gaze of his bright blue eyes. 'Hi,' I said warmly, and with outward confidence. 'You're Sean Whitmore, aren't you? I saw you in *Hamlet* this week.'

Sean's face broke into a broad grin. 'Yes, I know you did. You've been to every performance, haven't you?' Out of the corner of my eye I detected a you-didn't-tell-me-about-this expression on Melvyn's face, but thankfully he said nothing.

'You mean you could see me?' I was grinning inanely and my voice had taken on a sloppy, carefree tone. I managed to stop myself asking him to put his autograph on the back of my hand.

'We can see more from the stage than you think. But you made it very obvious by always sitting in the third row.' He had that easy, direct rapport that makes you feel as if you and everything you say are of the utmost importance. He probably made everybody feel like that, but I didn't care. I smiled back at him. Our eyes locked on each other. 'You must really like the play.'

I lowered my voice. 'I wasn't there for the play.'

He laughed. 'I sort of got the feeling you weren't.'

I feigned mock surprise: 'Really! I didn't realise I was being so obvious.' I was aware that I was still grinning and in a far-off sort of way I felt I was beginning to sound like a member of the Barry Manilow fan club. However, there was definitely a rapport between us and, flushed by my success so far, I pressed my prepared speech into action: 'I was wondering if you're doing anything after the performance tonight?' So bold.

'It's our last night in town and we all have to move on in the morning, so I'd kinda like to go out somewhere,' he replied. I had the feeling he was making it very easy for me.

'Well, that's great, because we're going to Club 49. Would you like to come?'

I had my mouth open but I didn't actually say those words. They came from Melvyn who was standing right beside me. 'Sorry, this is a friend of mine, Melvyn,' I said.

Although he shook hands with Melvyn, his eyes never left mine. This didn't seem to deter Melvyn, who carried on:

'It should be good fun. They're having a Judy Garland competition.'

'They're not!' Sean faced Melvyn directly.

Melvyn, always liking to sound an authority on things artistic, continued, 'They are. All you have to do is sing any one of her songs. I think the first prize is a weekend for two in Amsterdam.'

'You're joking!'

'Oh no,' stammered Melvyn. 'I'm quite serious.'

Sean took a step back and addressed us as if we were two theatrical agents. 'That's part of my act! I've got the whole costume, wigs and everything. There was a birthday party after the show last night for the company manager. We all crowded on stage and there was a disco, something to eat and some entertainment. I did it then as part of the cabaret. The *Trolley Song* from *Meet Me In St Louis*.' He paused for full dramatic impact. 'I'd love to re-create it for you both at the club.' He turned to face me again, lowering his voice as he spoke. 'And then maybe we could go on somewhere else afterwards?'

Words failed me. I opened my mouth. 'Oh,' I stammered. 'Oh. Oh.'

'Ophelia,' he replied. Melvyn laughed heartily – I expect it was the literary reference.

There was no problem picking Sean up from the theatre; after all, I had spent the rest of the day there watching the matinée and the evening performance. I have to admit I was taking the proceedings less than seriously, focusing more on what was going to happen later that evening than on what was taking place on stage. When Claudius announced half-way through the final performance, 'My words fly up, my thoughts remain below,' I was forced to agree with him. It seemed to take for ever before we got round to Hamlet taking the poison, although Sean didn't hang around when the curtain came down. He was changed and outside the stage door within ten minutes.

We arrived at the club to find Melvyn and his friend by the bar. 'Hello,' said Melvyn. 'This is my friend, Jonathan.'

Jonathan grinned and shook hands with us. He was wearing a large coat of the same type as Melvyn's and carried with him a large sports bag, presumably containing the Judy Garland costume, wig and make-up. Sean had left the theatre with something similar.

Sean offered to buy drinks and I was slightly surprised when he ordered a pint of lager and a double whisky chaser for himself. 'Dutch courage,' he said by way of explanation.

Jonathan said he'd just found out that all the competitors were to assemble back-stage in about half an hour.

'Are you in the competition too?' asked Sean.

'I am indeed,' cooed Jonathan. 'I've got all Judy's records and the videos.'

Sean's eyes lit up and the two of them went into an intricate and very complicated conversation about all the possibilities they had rejected before choosing the song they were going to sing. By the time they'd finished, several more drinks and double whisky chasers had been ordered, and I was beginning to feel increasingly left out of the conversation. Jonathan announced that he was going to sing *Born In A Trunk*, and it was all I could do to stop myself remarking that in that coat he looked as if he had been.

When the time arrived for them to make their way back-stage I was looking very sullen. Sean must have noticed because he gave me a kiss and a wink before saying, 'Won't be long.' Jonathan asked Melvyn to look after his coat while he was back-stage; Melvyn's friends always wanted him to guard their coats. It was their equivalent to girls dancing round their handbags. I noticed that Jonathan was wearing a Judy For Ever tee-shirt several sizes too small, which made his chest muscles look huge. Sean ordered another double whisky, waved us goodbye and disappeared back-stage with it and Jonathan.

I don't know if you've ever sat through twenty-five Judy Garland impersonations – it's very boring and the event wasn't even enlivened by Sean's performance. He didn't come on until very near the end, and he didn't look anything like Judy Garland. He just looked silly and slightly over the top, nowhere near as attractive as he was when he appeared in his Hamlet costume. Jonathan, on the other hand, looked very attractive. His act was, I thought, a lot more inventive than Sean's, although I have to say that the audience roared its approval at both of them. It was approaching two o'clock before the winner was announced. The compère grabbed the mike to inform us of the judges' decision. He announced the results in reverse order, and when he got to second place he cleared his throat loudly. We all jumped. 'Ladies and gentlemen, this is a sensation,' he yelled. 'The judges have decided, and I'm sure you'll agree with them, that there is a tie for first place. The winners of the Bring Back Judy competition are Jonathan Knight and Sean Whitmore.'

Jonathan and Sean, like all the other contestants, had changed out of their costumes. The audience broke out into loud cheering; it was obviously a popular decision. From my seat a few tables back I saw that Sean looked quite small standing next to Jonathan. Although flushed with success he seemed to be swaying slightly, as if he were having trouble standing up. Some of his reactions to the crowd's applause were loud and rather slurred, and I noticed how pale he looked under the stage lights of the club. The toil of the day was obviously catching up with him.

Jonathan seemed to take it much more in his stride. The tee-shirt accentuated the leanness of his body, and, as they embraced in a victory hug, I noticed how muscular and firm his arms were when compared to the stodgy thickness of Sean's. At last the applause and cheering died down and Sean leaned over to the compère and whispered something in his ear.

'Well, that's real cute,' the compère said into the microphone. 'Folks, the boys here wish it to be known that they're going to share the prize and see Amsterdam together.'

I threw in the towel then. The sight of Sean and Jonathan posing for photographs, their arms round each other holding a pair of tickets to Amsterdam in their free hands, sort of stuck in my throat. 'I'm going home; I'll ring you tomorrow,' I shouted to Melvyn above the din.

He looked surprised. 'What about Sean?' he asked.

'He is a dull and muddy-mettled rascal,' I replied.

And if you want to know where that comes from, go see *Hamlet*.

PICTURES OF SAND

Dave Royle

The trouble we run into when we're not looking where we're going.

It's ten fifteen on a cold Saturday morning in late November. The three of them sit in the shopping-mall car park waiting for Trina to show. The heater vents breathe hot air onto their faces but it's still cold inside the car. Karen rubs a tissue across the misty car window and looks towards the car park barrier, her snub nose squashed against the cold glass. The squeak of the tissue makes Hadyn laugh from the back seat.

'Eek, eek!' he mimics, giggling. Martin is fumbling for something in the glove compartment. Karen looks round. Hadyn has undone his dungarees and is sitting in his *Jungle Book* underpants with Granny's old string bag tied round his head like a huge floppy hair-net.

'Oh look, Martin,' Karen says. 'Look what Hadyn's done with Mum's old string bag!' Martin glances in the rear-view mirror. Karen notices he hasn't turned to see. 'You daft article!' she tells the child. Appreciating his new audience, Hadyn shakes his head one way, then another, until the string bag flies off and hits Martin on the back of the head. Karen laughs again. 'I wish we'd brought the camera. . .'

'Ar-ti-cle,' Hadyn says slowly, as if the word were a sweet to curl your tongue round.

'We may as well get out and wait for them by the barrier,' she says. 'You get off and meet us in the restaurant later.'

Martin watches a family tumble from the open doors of the car in front of them: mother, father and two red-faced children, all dressed in identical grey anoraks. They lock up and hurry, in a chattering huddle, towards the shopping-mall doors.

'Will you recognise her car?' he says, as Karen dresses Hadyn.

'Of course I will,' she says, not looking up. 'It's bright red. I should know my own sister's car.'

'All right – I only asked.' It's like this all the time now. A police car slides past the barrier and draws to a halt by the main doors.

'There's something going on,' Martin says. Karen and Hadyn are outside the car now, their hands clinging together in the cold. 'Will you be all right?' he hears himself ask her. Karen narrows her eyes. 'As if you care,' he imagines her saying. A wisp of white breath escapes from her mouth and disappears against the sky. 'See you later.'

Martin is a beautiful man. His face is fresh and open and honest-looking, his body big and comforting just to look at. He attracts women and men equally because they know, when they look at him, that what you see is what you get. He has no enemies. Karen has never told anyone but her sister what happened the first time she met Martin – that Friday night in the pub after work. He was standing by the window, watching his mate stab at the flashing buttons of a fruit machine. 'See him over there?' she'd said to one of the other girls. 'He's the sort who could make me have a spontaneous orgasm.'

'Karen!' her friend had said, giggling loudly. 'You surprise me.' She'd surprised herself. When he'd looked straight at her, she'd whispered to herself, 'Oh yes. . .' From then on she couldn't take her eyes off him. While the others fussed around, buying drinks and dragging spare chairs across the room, she'd sat staring at him. It had taken her precisely seven minutes to reach orgasm. After that, it was inevitable they'd end up married.

Martin stops at a bookshop on the way home. The window features copies of a large, hardback book open at various pages. Above the display hangs a photograph of a woman he recognises from the TV news, her thin lips closed in a tight smile. The woman seems to nod to him as the photo swings backwards and forwards in the warm air behind the window.

117

He looks at the photographs. One in particular draws his attention. He can tell it's early morning because the sea and sky glow dark and the sand is almost a rusty pink. It reminds him of their honeymoon, when they fucked at daybreak by the water's edge. In the foreground is a roll of barbed wire, overtaken by the tendrils of a plant with bright green, pear-shaped leaves. In the distance, beyond the curve of the coastline, tall buildings stand fuzzy against the dark sky.

He buys a packet of Christmas cards and two copies of the book. He may give one to Karen; the other will do for Ricky who had an empty space on the coffee table the last time he called round. The woman behind the counter tells him: 'If you'd like your copies signed, the author's appearing at our branch in the shopping mall this morning.' Martin notices the strange look she gives him, as if she half-recognises him from somewhere.

Trina has her chestnut hair piled up behind a stretchy black hairband. She's wearing skiing pants, a baggy black pullover under a grey jacket and plastic cube ear-rings that dangle to her shoulders. Karen looks for traces of make-up on Trina's face but she can't see any. What she has noticed, in the fifteen minutes they've been sitting at the corner table, is a stream of husbands and boyfriends glancing surreptitiously at her sister as they pass along the self-service queue.

'It's not a question of wrong,' she tells Karen. 'You're not doing anything wrong. It's just a phase.'

'But he doesn't seem to want us any more,' Karen tells her. 'He doesn't talk, he doesn't listen. It's like having another child around dragging his heels a few steps behind you the whole time.'

Trina gives her sister one of those looks Karen remembers from their childhood. Even her voice has a familiar ring of something close to vague contempt: 'Of course he wants you! What else would a man like Martin want? You're the envy of most people I know – including me, and I've told you that often enough.'

'What do you know?' Karen says, irritably. 'You're as bad as him! You don't listen to what I say. He's not the man I married. We may as well live apart – it couldn't be worse than this!'

118

Trina reaches across the table and touches her sister's tear-stained face. 'Little one. . .' she whispers.

Karen hunches over the shiny table-top. 'Oh Trina,' she sobs, 'if there was another woman I might understand. But I know there isn't.'

It seems strange at home without the others. The living room looks empty, though Hadyn's toys are piled in their usual corner by the TV, and the sofa is stacked with dusty boxes of Christmas decorations. It's just that without the others, nothing in the house seems to belong to him. He sits on the edge of the bed and dials Ricky's number. Four rings, then a click, the opening bars of *Land Of Hope and Glory*, then a woman's low, carefully modulated voice: 'Hello, this is Margaret Thatcher, ex-Prime Minister speaking. I'm afraid Ricky's. . .' How he hates that message. Where is he? Still asleep? Out shopping? At the launderette, washing his football kit from last night's match? It frightens Martin the way Ricky looks at him. Ricky fixes his eyes on him and never looks away, as if the older man might just disappear when the boy's back is turned. And Ricky's friends – the ones he's met – look at him in the same way. Will that change now? Will it get worse? More than once Ricky's referred to Martin's decision as "applying for a transfer." It seems to amuse him and the others, in the same way the novelty phone message amuses them.

After the first time at Ricky's flat, he'd returned home with dried cum round his wedding ring. He'd noticed it in the hall and rubbed it away on the sleeve of his pullover. But Karen wouldn't have noticed anyway: she was curled up on the sofa with the light off, her face bathed in flickering blue light from the TV screen, a mug of hot chocolate cupped in her small hands. She'd scarcely looked round and he'd noticed how the constantly moving, artificial light carved dark lines beneath her eyes.

Martin fills the suitcase with the first things he finds in the wardrobe. He doesn't even think about what he hasn't taken, what may be in the laundry basket or drying on radiators around the house, though he does remember to pack one decent shirt for Ricky's frequent dinner parties. On the way out he stops for a moment by the hall table

119

and considers leaving a note. Instead he goes to the car and brings the packet of Christmas cards indoors. Inside one card he writes 'I'm sorry – Martin,' and seals it in an envelope. At the last moment, he slips this into his jacket pocket and leaves the house.

Martin fights his way through the crowds by the mall door and hurries past the bookshop. Only a few people glance at the window display as they move in their great tidal wave of shell-suits and pastel-coloured winter anoraks towards the central aisle. He sees Karen waiting for him by the café door up on the atrium, her nervous, pinched face searching the faces below her. He swerves to the edge of the crowd and keeps close to the shop doorways, pausing finally by the open door of a cosmetics shop. When she moves her head, her bobbed hair swings like a shiny curtain above her shoulders. She looks very small. As he watches her, he thinks: this is the woman I stick my cock into. She looks after me when I'm ill; she hears me fart and shit when I don't shut the bathroom door. And for a split second he has that feeling again – the one he had when he first saw Ricky in the shower – like a pin racing down inside his dick.

Trina is still at the table, talking to a young woman dressed in a Santa Claus outfit. There's a clipboard in front of them and the woman is writing things on a sheet of paper.

'Did you get it all?' Karen asks him.

'Yes. Who's she?'

Santa is tapping her pen on the desk and staring towards the ceiling. Trina is still talking.

'She's interviewing us to find the perfect shopping family.' She notices the look on his face. 'Yeah, it's a bit of a joke, really, isn't it?'

The silence between them is horrible. He summons up courage. 'I want to say something.'

She purses her lips. 'Not now,' she says, inclining her head towards the table. 'She'll want to have a word with you.'

'But. . .'

Trina has seen them. She beckons them over, her earrings bouncing like square yo-yos from her ears. 'This is my brother-in-law Martin,' she tells the woman. 'He's been organising some kind of Christmas surprise for Karen and

120

Hadyn.' Santa looks Martin up and down and gives him a toothy smile.

'Ooh!' she says. Trina thinks to herself: you're fucking dangerous, Martin. Do you know that?

'I'd love to see you all together,' the girl says, 'with. . .' she glances down at her clipboard, a fleeting look of panic crossing her face '. . . Handel?'

'Hadyn,' Karen says, flatly. She searches in her bag and brings out a crumpled draw ticket, which she hands to Martin. 'Go and fetch him.'

'Karen, I. . .'

'Please, Martin. We're running late as it is. We've got Mum's Aquavac to buy yet.'

'Sod Mum's bloody Aquavac!'

Santa's pen hovers uncertainly over the sheet of paper. Trina coughs.

'Go and fetch him, Martin,' she says, soothingly. 'He'll be wondering where we are. We stopped too long to see that news reporter at the bookshop. We wondered what was going on, what with the police being here and everything.'

'Oh, they weren't here for her,' Santa tells her. 'We thought there might be a . . . well, let's call it a sort of demonstration here this morning.' She shifts uneasily in her chair.

'Well, it was a waste of time anyway!' Karen retorts.

'I thought the book was very interesting,' Santa says, trying to make her voice sound cultured. 'The photos really made me . . . well, think.'

'They didn't make me think,' Karen says, looking once again into her bag, as if she's searching for something. 'They were so ugly. Just pictures of sand and bombed buildings.'

Martin walks away, the draw ticket disintegrating between his hot fingers. He grabs the child's shoulder. Suddenly, Ricky is all he can think of: Ricky in his shiny blue football shorts, Ricky's thighs caked in mud, Ricky writing at his desk, his hair and forehead highlighted by the anglepoise lamp on the edge of the cluttered bookshelf. The child seems reluctant; he's holding back. Martin grips the small shoulder ever more tightly and pulls him forward, weaving between the lingering families with their bags and bags and bags of shopping. A small group has assembled near the entrance to the lift under the atrium. The edge of what looks like a banner waves slowly above their heads.

Karen and Trina are leaning over the table, their backs towards the door. Santa seems to be showing them photographs. She looks up and smiles as Martin approaches with the child. Then her expression changes to a puzzled frown. The two sisters turn round. Santa stares at him, a frown spoiling the smooth skin of her face like a blemish on a peach; Trina watches him, her mouth open in an almost perfect O; Karen, eyes dark and teeth clenched behind thin white lips, opens her mouth as if to speak, but says nothing. 'Happy families!' he says.

Trina attempts to speak but all she can manage is a strangled gurgle. Karen moves forward slightly, her hand resting on the table. 'Who the fuck is that?' She's looking down at the child by Martin's side.

The girl has curly, fair hair and the remains of a chocolate bar around her mouth. She's shaking and looks frightened. Trina sits down.

'Oh my God!' Karen is gripping the edge of the table. 'You stupid fucking idiot! Don't you even know your own child?' Santa is frantically doodling flowers around the edge of her clipboard, her blonde hair falling across her face. Martin opens his mouth but doesn't say anything. There are tears in Karen's dark eyes. 'Oh Martin,' she says, 'how could you?'

The child starts crying and wets the café floor.

Martin trips two steps from the ground and collides with the edge of a banner. A young man with greased-back hair and a mustard-coloured woolly jacket is smiling into his face. 'Come and join us, big boy,' he says, smiling. His breath smells of sherry. Martin looks up at the banner above the boy's head – "We're here, we're queer and we're not stoppin' shoppin'!" Someone shouts something abusive and a half-eaten burger hits the banner. A trickle of tomato sauce drops from the banner onto the shoulder of the boy's jacket. 'Fuckin' wanker!' Someone else is pushing towards him. The newcomer rests his hand on the boy's sauce-splashed shoulder. Martin wants to run but he can't move.

'Martin!' Ricky is wearing his favourite blue flight jacket and tight jeans with his cock and balls jammed down one leg. His hair has been razored at the sides and gelled into a narrow quiff on top. Martin doesn't say anything. 'Fuck me!' Ricky says, turning to his friend. 'This is Martin!'

'Fuckin' bona!'

Then he touches Martin's arm. 'Have you done it?' he asks, frowning suddenly. Martin nods. Ricky smiles and moves to embrace him, but Martin darts smartly away just as four police officers move in. 'Stay out of this,' Ricky says. 'You've got the spare key. Make yourself at home and I'll be back soon. Don't worry about me.'

Martin runs. He parks in the usual place, two streets from Ricky's flat and picks up a copy of the book from the passenger seat beside him. The smooth pages still smell of ink. He turns to a photograph of Northern Ireland. In the foreground is a winding country lane with a huge crater in it. All the trees and hedges around the crater have been blown to bits. Further along the road, a little plastic tent conceals something lying on the stained tarmac. The countryside dips and climbs away from the road towards a jagged, treeless horizon. Far in the distance, exposed against the skyline, is the shape of what looks like a solitary figure bending slightly towards the ground.

He hauls the suitcase from the back seat and locks the car. A brass band is playing carols in the Old Market Square a few streets away. It doesn't feel like Christmas. A dozen silver baubles, suspended from the light fitting, clink as he opens the door. Ricky has left a scrawled message on the stairs: 'Welcome home, Tiger! I'll be back mid-p.m. We're invited out to dinner tonite. XX.' Martin re-reads the note a few times, then takes the sealed envelope from his jacket pocket. He writes Ricky's name on the front and leaves it on the hall table beside the spare key. Then he goes back to the car and drives to the phone box in the Old Market Square just as the rain begins.

Trina removes Hadyn's coat and scarf while Karen jams herself onto the sofa and presses the replay button on the answering machine. Martin's voice, muffled by the sound of a brass band and rain drumming against plastic, sounds far-off and unhappy. She begs Trina to drive her immediately to the Old Market. Trina persuades her to sit tight, amidst the boxes overflowing with tinsel and crushed streamers, and wait for him to come home. But Martin, driving hard through the November rain, has left all of them behind for ever.

A TRANSFORMATION

Paul Brownsey

I called him Foetus Head; an unsubtle name, you might think, but that was part of the reason it fitted him, for *he* was unsubtle as he padded up and down the hot rooms of the Turkish baths. As you reclined on a bench in the baking dry heat, you were likely to find, sooner or later, that Foetus Head had halted before you, an inane conspiratorial grin on his over-large, unlinked, coarse-featured face; then he would unwrap his towel to display his large but featureless cock. Pointedly turning away your eyes and head, as I did, never discouraged him, for (even if there were others in the room besides you and him) he would then take hold of his cock and start rubbing it, all the while looking as delighted as if he had met with the response anyone could desire. I sometimes entertained the thought that he had no conception that sex might consist of anything other than his playing with himself in the face of the aloof turning away he got from me and all the others I saw him approach; but that was a silly thought, since he could not have failed to witness sex at the baths that was joint and mutually eager.

Then there was Health and Efficiency. The man to whom I gave this name had a worn, late-middle-aged face, with short thick white hair above, and forward-pointing grey sideburns that might once have been raffish; but he had, too, amazingly, the perfect man's body (nothing boyish about it, nor was it merely well-preserved) of someone, oh, twenty-five years younger; and he never wore a towel but stood around ostenta-tiously naked, adopting old-fashioned poses that declared the health-giving benefits of nudity in the fresh air and sunshine: hand low on hip, for instance, one leg pointed forward, and head thrown back as if to catch the ocean breeze beneath his chin. (He might have caught some gasps of hot air from the vent in the wall.) Usually he behaved as if he were oblivious of the rest of us and were wholly absorbed in health-promoting exercises: he would go in for deep breathing, his eyes shut as though he were monitoring the quantity and quality of the health that accrued to him thereby, or he would run on the spot, straining his knees very high indeed (as if he had a target to reach) while his unusually large balls bounced and his eyes had the far-away look of someone trying to recall and translate into action a complicated exercise programme that *must* be adhered to. I used to wonder whether the performance was an attempt to persuade himself that he only went to the baths for the sake of his health. His body sometimes tempted me, but when I raised my eyes to the grandfather's face atop it I lost all incentive to try to break in on his self-absorption, real or pretended.

Mister Seedy, whom I first encountered in the steam room in the form of a hand, its owner, invisible in the steam, fumbling at the join of the towel I had around me, I so named because he wasn't merely a bit pathetic, a bit hopeless, a bit seedy, in this or that respect: to me he was seediness personified, the Mister Man of seediness, animated by nothing but pure seediness from the shape of his glasses to the hang of his thin buttocks. Of course I hadn't yet named him, that day of the disembodied hand in the steam. I leaned in its direction sufficiently to enable me to discern that its owner was unattractive, and then I brought my fist down hard on it, angling my blow so that the large ring I wore might hurt him, and said, 'Fuck off!'

Later, as I sat in the coolest of the hot rooms reading a selection of Housman, he came and stood indecisively by the wooden armchair next to mine. I gave no indication of having noticed him and pretended to continue to read. Eventually he sat down, his gaze towards the opposite wall, and said forlornly, 'Were you the one that told me to fuck off in the steam room?'

'That depends,' I said, delivering the line well, 'on whether more than one person is going around sticking his hand up towels uninvited.' To drive home the rebuke I pretended to adjust my steel-rimmed glasses and returned my eyes, though not my concentration, to Housman.

Some minutes later, musingly, as if he had not noticed my rebuke, Mister Seedy went on, 'You see, you're different. Not like the *queers* who hang around down here. They're scum.' He still looked towards the opposite wall; you would have thought he was speaking to himself. 'What I did to you, it was awful. I lost control of myself. I'm ashamed I did it, to *you*. You're special. Different.' I gave a gracious portmanteau nod, intended to signify that I agreed I was special and different, that I accepted his apology, and that the interview was now at a close. Suddenly he turned to me and said pleadingly, 'Don't look at me like I've crawled out from under a stone. I've got feelings, too. We all have. *I* can appreciate you, even if these' – a noun eluded him, but he gestured towards Foetus Head, just then lumbering through, his large head swaying as if the effort to keep it upright were very great – 'can't. I've always wanted to meet a friend like you, though of course you only meet rubbish down here. Still, beggars can't be choosers. So, you know, is it all right if I. . .?' As his eyes completed the enquiry his hand moved rather swiftly towards the join in my towel, pausing inches away, and I was surprised to find that the thought of permitting Mister Seedy to have his way with me, or some of it, suddenly appealed. Of course, I was repelled by him, but that was how a rent boy must often feel about his clients: it might be interesting to experience myself in that light. I turned my gaze back to Housman, to indicate I expected nothing for myself from what was about to happen, but at the same time loosened the knot on my towel to indicate that I acceded to his plea.

Just then the door opened: someone new, young, with the confident masculinity of an irresistible tanned body in tension with a puzzled boyish face on which a wispy black moustache endearingly suggested that growing it might have taxed his puppyish strength. He cast a practised glance around the room, then undid and retied the towel round his middle; and he did it just like someone innocent of the fact that he thereby allowed me, and only me, a brief but sufficient view of a cock in excellent harmony with the rest of him. He backed out of the room as he finished tying the knot, his eyes fixed on me as if to draw me after him. 'Ah, but you'll be wanting him now,' said Mister Seedy. 'No one really wants someone like me, do they?' I was irritated that Mister Seedy should have discerned my interest in the newcomer. I always prided myself on keeping my enthusiasms concealed until *I* chose to disclose them, and this pride almost led me to contradict Mister Seedy and allow him to proceed with his grope, until I saw again in my mind's eye the slight arching movement, as he adjusted his towel, of the newcomer's nude brown body in profile – he had obviously got his tan in the nude, for it did not halt at the trunks area. I was irritated further by Mister Seedy's question, which seemed manipulatively designed to compel the reply that I, at least, wanted him. I said, 'Too bloody right,' laid down Housman, tied up my towel, and set off in pursuit of . . . well, I never did invent a name for him.

But it *was* an occupation, in those long hours at the Turkish baths, uncoupled from space and time, wholly outside the ordinary world of work and weather, of personal relationships and clothes, safe from antecedents and consequences, from the past and the future, even from myself, to think up names for the inmates. Sometimes on Joe-the-attendant's radio I would hear snatches of news broadcasts: a terrorist bomb had been found in London, interest rates were going up, a lorry had crashed on the M8 causing a big traffic tail-back. But what was all that to me? Nothing on the radio *really* applied to me, even though I might later have to drive along that same traffic-jammed M8 to get home. I was secure here, lulled by the steam and hot air, and my flesh was not vulnerable to a terrorist's bomb, and I gave myself to the desires and etiquette of a secret world; here I would stretch out on a grimy bench, sometimes conscious of the generations of heads that had been lowered onto the same spot (for I was intermittently anxious about infections), and evolve Foetus Head, Health And Efficiency or Job.

I was particularly pleased with Job. Its bearer was in his late thirties I suppose, with a skinny body and a curiously-shaped face, triangular and too small, beneath a flat top of boyish straight black hair. I surmised he was religious, for whereas others at the baths might read novels or newspapers or even (like me) poetry – I never saw anyone with a dirty magazine – he invariably held before him (though more often than not his eyes could be discerned peeping over the top of it) the current issue of *Life and Work*. His being religious was one reason why the name of an Old Testament worthy fitted him. Further, the available space on his little face was always crowded with spots and pimples, and there were even, so I thought, pimples on pimples, the whole a plague of Egyptian boils sent by a testing Jehovah. He avoided all eye contact, maintaining a pained, narrow, abstracted look on his face as if he were listening to harrowing private music or, as I liked to think, reliving the loss of his herds of camels. He wore his large towel across his shoulders and held the ends crossed in front of him, so that it looked like some sort of desert garment; and he walked humbly, with head bent (though you could see his eyes glitter upwards.) Altogether, "Job" was perfect. He was a lurker and a watcher. I never knew him to have, or signal willingness to have, or be invited to have, sex with anyone, but where two or three were gathered together, as they thought privately, to feel and suck and occasionally to try to fuck, there you might find Job, not in the midst of them but to one side, turned away from the participants with his head lowered, as though engrossed in theodicy, but sliding his eyes towards the participants and away again; a witness for the Lord, perhaps.

Some names, though, I couldn't get right, and this irked me. Desmond Disdain, for instance, I couldn't see how to improve, nor could I think of an alternative; yet it lacked playfulness, resonance, a cutting edge. I pondered turning it into some variant of Desdemona – Disdainmona, say; but that was too clumsy and convoluted, and only a proven taste for black guys on the part of its bearer, which I had no reason to suppose he had, would have led me to persist with my name-honing in that direction. The crudely female Doris Disdain would be a name with spite and punch, but then it wouldn't fit *him*, for there was nothing womanish about him. He was a thin blond guy with a hunted face and "Des" in a scroll, tattooed on his left forearm. There had been sex between us several times at the baths. The initiative was always his: say, we would be lying on adjacent benches in an otherwise empty, hot room and he would undo his towel and start fondling his cock (though staring at the ceiling as if this were a wholly private function); yet when I responded, getting to my feet and substituting my hand for his in the fondling, he would look at me disdainfully, as if I were a tiresome supplicant whom he was humouring only reluctantly, who really should know better, whom he was not going to assist in the slightest. He lay wholly inert throughout, arms by his sides, palms down on the bench, his eyes seeking from mine an acknowledgement of the needlessness of what was taking place; and he even came with disdain on his face. Nor did he ever speak. Once, to see what would happen, I said, 'I'd like to see you outside;' all that happened was that his look of disdain changed into a fully-fledged sneer, as though, after previously leaving room for doubt, I had finally given incontrovertible proof of my degradation. But he was no less keen to invite my attentions the next time we met at the baths, and when, initially, I did not respond, he even showed signs of bafflement and dismay, as if I had welshed on a standing agreement. Beneath it all, I told myself, he was probably a nice guy; but then, it was easy to tell yourself that about anyone you fancied.

No doubt sooner or later I'd have told myself that about the puppyish newcomer who had intruded on me and Mister Seedy. Having hurried from the hot rooms in pursuit of him, however, I was now perplexed to know where he had gone. The steam room was to the right; ahead were the showers (no curtains: the authorities had removed them because too often there was double occupancy of the cubicles formed by the curtains), and to the left were the stairs. One flight led upwards to the changing room, where the presence of Joe-the-attendant gave no opportunity for sex; my newcomer seemed experienced enough to have thought of that, so I guessed he was not up there. A second flight led down to the basement, known to us as the catacombs. All that was supposed to be of concern to us down there was the toilet, a single cubicle with a door which the authorities had rendered unlockable, but a number of other rooms led off the cold, dirty, dimly-lit, concrete-floored corridor; rooms which, so far as I could tell, were not in official use and which, amazingly, were unlocked. Two contained ancient baths, though no water ran from the taps; two contained hot-air vents and were perhaps former drying-rooms for laundry; others contained stacks of boxes, old timber and bricks, assorted junk, all bearing years of dust. In a couple of rooms the lights still worked; in others you could see only by leaving the door ajar to admit a little of the corridor's dim light. Here amidst the forgotten debris and dirt (your feet got black just standing there) you could have sex in private. On the rare occasions when a shod footstep announced that a baths employee was somewhere about, you could always formulate the plea (notwithstanding the erections visible through your towels) that the pair (or more) of you were looking for the toilet.

My newcomer wasn't in the showers. Desmond Disdain was, washing his hair, and he caught my glance and curled his lip at me, as if he had divined my quest and was deprecating it, but of course he always gave such looks. Most likely my newcomer was in the catacombs, and the thought of his body awaiting me down there was exciting. But first I checked that he was not in the steam room, and I made the circuit of its steam-shrouded, hunched-together occupants, peering at them while trying not to seem to do so. My exit was barred by the sudden appearance in the doorway of Robbie Coltrane: not *the* Robbie Coltrane, of course, but a lookalike whose resemblance to the actor lay not only in his bulk and his face but also in his potentially sly look and his surprising capacity for daintiness. So huge was his middle that not even the big towel supplied by the baths could be joined round it, and he held the towel in place with both hands while gripping an inflated plastic pillow, pink with black spots, beneath his elbow. My attempt to push past him was unavailing. 'Manners!' he cried reprovingly, without budging from the doorway, and his voice modulated into the poshest Kelvinside drawl to add, 'For fuck's sake!'

Impatiently I said, 'O.K., sorry,' but he would not let me off yet.

'D'you like my footwear?' He raised each massive leg in turn to display it; a voice from the steam cried, 'Shut the fucking door!' but Robbie ignored it. 'They're flip-flops. Flip-flops. So onomatopoeic. And such reliable protection against athlete's foot, fungus of the toes, and much else. Here's my advice, young man. Get yourself a pair. You have the body for them. You'd be *such* a turn-on in flip-flops. But a word of warning: flip-flops do not prevent infections Higher Up. Not if you wear them where they should be worn, at any rate.' My polite smile had worn very thin, understandably, but this time he let me pass, although he made me squeeze by. Somehow I hadn't quite got my balance before I started down the stairs to the catacombs; I slipped or missed my footing, toppled, felt the hard bang of the concrete steps, and then realised I was lying on my back in the corridor at the foot of the stairs. People stood round me: I felt my shoulders lifted, and I was leaning against someone's knee. Surrounded by helping hands (even in my dazed and pained condition I was alert to the possibility that some of them might take the opportunity to paw or grope me, but I don't think any did), I hobbled up the stairs, and upstairs again to the changing room. My right knee was very painful; and I collapsed onto a chair in the lounge area. Robbie Coltrane had already commandeered the attendant's kettle (Joe was nowhere to be seen) and was filling it at the sink. He said, 'I'm doing my district nurse act, and what I prescribe is hot sweet tea. Hot sweet *me* you'll have to postpone to another time;' but the campery of his words evaporated in the kindliness of his smile.

As I sipped my tea, still dazed, I became aware of Foetus Head, his arm extended, something held out to me. My glasses! They must have flown off in my fall and one of the arms was now badly bent; had I landed on them? As I reached for them he raised a finger to signal 'Wait,' and, kneeling before me, began to unbend the crooked arm. 'Don't worry – I used to have a vacation job at Western Optical when I was at Uni,' he said in a quiet, precise voice that exuded authority and compelled trust. Without hesitating he sat the glasses on me, his delicate controlled fingertips brushing the sides of my head and the tips of my ears, an oddly comforting sensation if you didn't think beyond it. 'Look me straight in the eyes,' he ordered; I couldn't do that: my gaze flinched from the unknown intelligence in his pupils and I attached it instead to his lower eyelids; I could feel his surprisingly sweet breath on my face. 'Right,' he said, removing the glasses and doing some more bending and shaping. He returned them to my face (his fingertips against my ears again): they fitted perfectly. Startled, I expressed my thanks. 'No problem,' he said, patting my uninjured knee in pure friendly reassurance, so far as I could judge. He padded away downstairs.

I got to my feet intending to make for my locker; my knee buckled under me and I gasped with pain. I saved myself from falling only by grabbing the back of the chair. Mister Seedy emerged from the lockers in the process of putting his clothes on; there was an extensive yellow stain in the pouch of his over-large white underpants. He spoke brusquely: 'You'd better get down to Casualty. I've got my car – want a lift? I won't be able to stay while they look at you, though – the wife's expecting me home.' Surely that couldn't be *delicacy* from Mister Seedy, his way of intimating that nothing but a lift in his car was being offered? So engrossing was the question that my 'O.K.' was off-hand and sounded as if I were doing *him* a favour.

I hobbled to my locker and started to dress. Trailing his towel ostentatiously behind him, Health and Efficiency proudly walked the length of the changing room. It transpired that I was his destination. He threw out his chest and composed his face, so far as its unyouthful coarseness allowed, in an expression of hearty, innocent masculine chumminess; this compelled a doubtful answering pause in me, and we stood together, him naked and me in only briefs, as if posing for a locker-room photograph in which comradeship and fitness were to mask the sexual sub-text. Then he held out a card on which was what I took to be his name. Hamish L. Bruce, and the name of a firm of lawyers, Cullen Bruce. His voice was careful and wise. 'I've taken a look at that stair. That stair-covering – it's not properly attached at the top – no wonder you slipped. You could have a case there. Get a bit of cash for yourself and get the bloody Council to take an interest in this place; that way we'll all benefit. Don't make the claim too big and they probably won't even contest it. Anyway, think about it. Give me a bell if you want to follow it up.'

Health and Efficiency had conjured up a scenario that appealed to me. In me the Council would find they had to deal, not with one of the meek and furtive inmates, shrinking from any fuss that might have a connection, however tenuous, with his desires, but with a self-confident gay man unashamed of his sexuality and prepared to outface the officials. Yet I knew I would not in reality pursue the matter, for how could I explain the correspondence, and the money, to my lover, Alex? And anyway, did I really want the Council to take an interest in the baths which might lead to their taking an interest in what went on there?

Mister Seedy was waiting for me at the exit; yes, his raincoat *was* dirty. He spoke almost angrily as he preceded me out the door: 'You'd better get a move on. We're late.' I wondered whether to correct him: *he* might be late but I wasn't; then he turned and smiled (though still seedily) and his tone softened. 'But I don't suppose you *can* hurry, can you?' As I reached to pull the door behind me Desmond Disdain caught my eye. He called 'Bye,' smiled warmly and waved, like an old friend, and I smiled and waved back, as if indeed he were. It was a transformation.

The Contributors

Paul Brownsey has for twenty years lived and taught in the West of Scotland.

Martin Foreman's first novel, *Weekend*, was published by Third House in 1990 and was reprinted in 1991. A collection of his short stories, *A Sense of Loss*, is being published by GMP in November 1992. He lives in London.

Charles Lambert was born and educated in England. He now lives in Rome, where he works as a teacher and translator. A story of his, *Money*, was published in *The Freezer Counter* (Third House, 1989.)

Paul Mann spent two years in the Royal Marines by mistake, eleven years at sea by choice and does little now other than read and write. His story, *The Park Job*, was published in *Messr Rondo* (GMP, 1983.)

Love and Onions is the first story Phillip McKew has written. Aged twenty-nine, he designs and runs training courses for a living. He lives in Harrow.

Joe Mills has had stories published in *Gay Scotland*, *Oranges and Lemons* (Third House, 1987), *The Freezer Counter*, and *The Ten Commandments* (Serpent's Tail, 1992.) His first novel, *Towards the End*, was published in 1990 by Polygon, and he has just completed a second, *Eighteen*, which is about a boy with the biggest penis in the world.

Chris Payne lives in South London. His stories have been published in *Cracks In The Image* (GMP, 1982), *Oranges and Lemons* and *The Freezer Counter*.

Edwin Preece lives in Hertfordshire. His story, *The Freezer Counter*, was published in the anthology of that name.

David Rees's autobiography, *Not For Your Hands*, was published in 1992 by Third House to considerable critical acclaim. Author of some forty books, he is best-known for *The Exeter Blitz*, a novel for children which won the Carnegie Medal in 1978, and the best-selling *The Milkman's On His Way* (GMP, 1982.)

Peter Robins lives in London. He has had four collections of short stories and four novels published. Six of his plays have been staged or broadcast. His most recent book, *Visits*, was published by Third House in 1992.

Dave Royle was born in London but grew up in Suffolk. He worked for some years in magazine journalism and now writes full-time. His first collection of short stories, *Pleasing the Punters*, was published by Third House in 1990. He is currently working on a number of writing projects, including two novels.

Alexander Wakelin works in architectural conservation. At the age of thirty, he is starting to write fiction, mainly to make himself feel human. *True Colours* is his first published story.

Michael Wilcox's stage plays include *Rents*, *Accounts*, *Lent*, and *Green Fingers*. His television credits include *Crown Court*, *Inspector Morse*, and film versions of *Lent* and *Accounts*. *Outlaw in the Hills*, an autobiographical account of a gay playwright's year, was published by Methuen in 1991.